INCREDIBLE
COWBOY
STORIES

T0056761

INCREDIBLE COWBOY STORIES

AMAZING TALES OF WESTERN DANGER AND DERRING-DO

EDITED BY VERONICA ALVARADO

Skyhorse Publishing

Skyhorse Publishing books may be purchased in bulk at special discounts for sales promotion, corporate gifts, fund-raising, or educational purposes. Special editions can also be created to specifications. For details, contact the Special Sales Department, Skyhorse Publishing, 307 West 36th Street, 11th Floor, New York, NY 10018 or info@skyhorsepublishing.com.

Skyhorse® and Skyhorse Publishing® are registered trademarks of Skyhorse Publishing, Inc.®, a Delaware corporation.

Visit our website at www.skyhorsepublishing.com.

10 9 8 7 6 5 4 3 2

Library of Congress Cataloging-in-Publication Data is available on file.

Cover design by Tom Lau
Cover photo credit: iStockphoto

Print ISBN: 978-1-5107-3222-3
Ebook ISBN: 978-1-5107-3227-8

Printed in China.

TABLE OF CONTENTS

INTRODUCTION

When one thinks of truly American archetypes, a handful of distinct personas come to mind: the revolutionary minuteman; the founding father; the intrepid explorer; but perhaps none is more iconic than the cowboy of the Wild West. Strong and silent, equipped with a deft hand whether lassoing cattle or aiming a gun, and always brimming with courage and a touch of bravado, the cowboy is a symbolic piece of American culture.

So it should come as no surprise that a there is an entire literary canon devoted to extolling the allure of the icon of the Wild West.

This book contains a handful of those great Western tales, culled from a variety of sources and authored by some of the greatest writers of the genre. The first section, "Cowboys as Writers" showcases scenes penned directly by cowboys. Pieces included here come from legendary bounty hunter Charles Siringo, who describes his first lessons in cow wrangling, and cattleman Andy Adams, who details part of a long cattle drive. Despite stark sentences and straightforward style, these pieces provide readers with the greatest insight into the West as it once as.

The middle section, "Cowboy Chroniclers," contains selections from writers who, although they did not consider themselves to be cowboys, lived in the West and amongst the people whose stories they recorded. Writers such as Emerson Hough, Walter Noble Burns, Clarence E. Mulford, and William MacLeod Raine are included here.

In addition to being great pieces of literature, these works are prime examples of the emergence of cowboy literature as a permanent chapter in American literature.

The final section, entitled "Classic Authors" showcases pieces by writers who are still—as of 2018, anyway—household names. Zane Grey and Max Brand, two of the most famous authors of the Western canon, are featured in this section, as are veritable American giants Theodore Roosevelt and Mark Twain.

With more than a dozen tales of Western lore, there's sure to be something for every reader, whether you are a city slicker, a tried-and-true Westerner, or somewhere in between. So giddy up and enjoy *Incredible Cowboy Stories*!

PART ONE

COWBOYS AS WRITERS

CHAPTER ONE

MY FIRST LESSON
IN COW PUNCHING

Charles Siringo

"Cattle Roundup," George B. Bonnell, circa 1890.

The next day after arriving in town, Mr. Faldien sent me out to his ranch, twenty miles, on Big Boggy. I rode out on the "grub" wagon with the colored cook. That night, after arriving at the ranch, there being several men already there, we went out wild boar hunting. We got back about midnight very tired and almost used up. Such a hunt was very different from the coon hunts Billy and I used to have at the "Settlement." Our dogs were badly gashed up by the boars, and it was a wonder some of us hadn't been served the same way.

In a few days Mr. Faldien came out to the ranch, bringing with him several men. After spending a few days gathering up the cow-ponies, which hadn't been used since the fall before, we started for Lake Austin—a place noted for wild cattle.

During the summer I was taken sick and had to go home. I was laid up for two months with typhoid fever. Everyone thought I would die.

That fall, about October, mother married a man by the name of Carrier, who hailed from Yankeedom. He claimed that he owned a farm in Michigan, besides lots of other property.

He was very anxious to get back to his farm, so persuaded mother to sell out lock, stock and barrel and go with him.

She had hard work to find a buyer as money was very scarce, but finally she got Mr. George Burkheart, a merchant in Matagorda, to set his own price on things and take them.

The house and one hundred and seventy-five acres of land only brought one hundred and seventy-five dollars. The sixty head of cattle that we had succeeded in getting back from the mainland went at one dollar a head and all others that still remained on the mainland—thrown in for good measure.

At last everything for sale was disposed of and we got "Chris" Zipprian to take us to Indianola in his schooner. We bade farewell to the old homestead with tears in our eyes. I hated more than anything else to leave old "Browny" behind for she had been a friend in need as well as a friend indeed. Often when I would be hungry and afraid to go home for fear of mother and the mush stick, she would let me go up to her on the prairie calf fashion and get my milk. She was nearly as old as myself.

At Indianola we took the Steamship *Crescent City* for New Orleans. The first night out we ran into a large Brig and came very near going under. The folks on the Brig were nearly starved to death, having been drifting about for thirty days without a rudder. We took them in tow, after getting our ship in trim again, and landed them safely in Galveston.

There was a bar-room on our ship, and our new lord and master, Mr. Carrier, put in his spare time drinking whisky and gambling; I do not think he drew a sober breath from the time we left Indianola until we landed in New Orleans, by that time he had squandered every cent received for the homestead and cattle, so mother had to go down into her stocking and bring out the little pile of gold which she had saved up before the war for "hard times," as she used to say. With this money she now bought our tickets to Saint Louis. We took passage, I think, on the "Grand Republic." There was also a bar-room on this boat, and after wheedling mother out of the remainder of her funds, he drank whisky and gambled as before, so we landed in Saint Louis without a cent.

Mother had to pawn her feather mattress and pillows for a month's rent in an old delapidated frame building on one of the back streets. It contained only four rooms, two upstairs and two down; the lower rooms were occupied by the stingy old landlord and family; we lived in one of the upper rooms, while a Mr. Socks, whose wife was an invalid, occupied the other.

The next day after getting established in our new quarters, the "old man," as I called him, struck out to find a job; he found one at a dollar a day shoveling coal.

At first he brought home a dollar every night, then a half and finally a quarter. At last he got to coming home drunk without a nickel in his pocket. He finally came up missing; we didn't know what had become of him. Mother was sick in bed at the time from worrying. I went out several times hunting work but no one would even give me a word of encouragement, with the exception of an old Jew who said he was sorry for me.

A little circumstance happened, shortly after the "old man" pulled his trifling carcass for parts unknown, which made me a better boy and no doubt a better man than I should have been had it never happened.

Everything was white without, for it had been snowing for the past two days. It was about five o'clock in the evening and the cold piercing north wind was whistling through the unceiled walls of our room. Mother was sound asleep, while sister and I sat shivering over an old, broken stove, which was almost cold, there being no fuel in the house.

Sister began crying and wondered why the Lord let us suffer so? I answered that may be it was because we quit saying our prayers. Up to the time we left Texas mother used to make us kneel down by the bed-side and repeat the Lord's Prayer every night before retiring. Since then she had, from worrying, lost all interest in Heavenly affairs.

"Let us say our prayers now, then, brother!" said sister, drying the tears from her eyes.

We both knelt down against the old, rusty stove and commenced. About the time we had finished the door opened and in stepped Mr. Socks with a bundle under his arm. "Here children, is a loaf of bread and some butter and I will bring you up a bucket of coal in a few moments, for I suppose from the looks of the stove you are cold," said the good man, who had just returned from his day's work.

Was ever a prayer so quickly heard? We enjoyed the bread and butter, for we hadn't tasted food since the morning before.

The next day was a nice sunny one, and I struck out up town to try and get a job shoveling snow from the sidewalks.

The first place I tackled was a large stone front on Pine Street. The kind lady of the establishment said she would give me twenty-five cents if I would do a good job cleaning the sidewalk in front of the house.

After an hour's hard work I finished, and, after paying me, the lady told me to call next day and she would give me a job shoveling coal down in the cellar, as I had done an extra good job on the sidewalk. This was encouraging and I put in the whole day shoveling snow, but never found any more twenty-five cent jobs; most I received for one whole hour's work was ten cents, and then the old fat fellow kicked like a bay steer, about the d—d snow being such an expense, etc.

From that time on I made a few dimes each day sawing wood or shoveling coal and therefore got along splendid.

I forgot to mention my first evening in Saint Louis. I was going home from the bakery when I noticed a large crowd gathered in front of a corner grocery; I went up to see what they were doing. Two of the boys had just gotten through fighting when I got there; the store-keeper and four or five other men were standing in the door looking on at the crowd of boys who were trying to cap another fight.

As I walked up, hands shoved clear to the bottom of my pockets, the store-keeper called out, pointing at me, "There's a country Jake that I'll bet can lick any two boys of his size in the crowd."

Of course all eyes were then turned onto me, which, no doubt, made me look sheepish. One of the men asked me where I was from; when I told him, the store-keeper exclaimed, "By gum, if he is from Texas I'll bet two to one that he can clean out any two boys of his size in the crowd."

One of the other men took him up and they made a sham bet of ten dollars, just to get me to fight. The two boys were then picked out; one was just about my size and the other considerably smaller. They never asked me if I would take a hand in the fight until everything was ready. Of course I hated to crawl out, for fear they might think I was a coward.

Everything being ready, the store-keeper called out, "Dive in boys!"

We had it up and down for quite a while, finally I got the largest one down, and was putting it to him in good shape, when the other one picked up a piece of brick-bat and began pounding me on the back of the head with it. I looked up to see what he was doing and he struck me over one eye with the bat. I jumped up and the little fellow took to his heels, but I soon overtook him and blackened both of his eyes up in good shape, before the other boy, who was coming at full tilt could get there to help him. I then chased the other boy back to the crowd. That ended the fight and I received two ginger-snaps, from the big hearted store-keeper, for my trouble. I wore the nick-name of "Tex" from that time on, during my stay in that neighborhood; and also wore a black eye, where the little fellow struck me with the bat, for several days afterwards.

About the middle of January mother received a letter from the "old man," with ten dollars enclosed, and begging her to come right on without delay as he had a good job and was doing well, etc. He was at Lebanon, Ill., twenty-five miles from the city. The sight of ten dollars and the inducements he held out made us hope that we would meet with better luck there, so we packed up our few traps and started on the Ohio and Mississippi railroad.

On arriving in Lebanon about nine o'clock at night we found the "old man" there waiting for us.

The next morning we all struck out on foot, through the deep snow, for Moore's ranch where the "old man" had a job chopping cord wood. A tramp of seven miles brought us to the little old log cabin which was to be our future home. A few rods from our cabin stood a white frame house in which lived Mr. Moore and family.

Everything went on lovely for the first week, notwithstanding that the cold winds whistled through the cracks in our little cabin, and we had nothing to eat but corn bread, black coffee and old salt pork that Moore could not find a market for.

The first Saturday after getting established in our new home the "old man" went to town and got on a glorious drunk, squandered every nickel he could rake and scrape; from that time on his visits to town were more frequent than his trips to the woods, to work. At last I was compelled to go to work for Moore at eight dollars a month, to help keep the wolf from our door, and don't you forget it, I earned eight dollars a month, working out in the cold without gloves and only half clothed.

Towards spring the "old man" got so mean and good-for-nothing that the neighbors had to run him out of the country. A crowd of them surrounded the house one night, took the old fellow out and preached him a sermon; then they gave him until morning to either skip or be hung. You bet he didn't wait until morning.

A short while afterwards mother took sister and went to town to hunt work. She left her household goods with one of the near neighbors, a Mr. Muck, where they still remain I suppose, if not worn out. But there was nothing worth hauling off except the dishes. I must say the table ware was good; we had gotten them from a Spanish vessel wrecked on the Gulf beach during the war.

Mother found work in a private boarding house, and sister with a Mrs. Bell, a miller's wife, while I still remained with Moore at the same old wages.

Along in June sometime I quit Moore on account of having the ague. I thought I should have money enough to take a rest until I got well, but bless you I only had ninety cents to my credit, Moore had deducted thirty-five dollars the "old man" owed him out of my earnings. I pulled for town as mad as an old setting hen. But I soon found work again, with an old fellow by the name of John Sargent, who was to give me eight dollars a month, board and clothes and pay my doctor bills.

About the first of September mother and sister went to Saint Louis where they thought wages would be higher. They bade me good bye, promising to find me a place in the city, so I could be with them; also promised to write.

Shortly afterwards I quit Mr. Sargent with only one dollar to my credit; and that I haven't got yet. He charged me up with everything I got in the shape of clothes, doctor bills, medicine, etc.

I then went to work for a carpenter, to learn the trade, for my board, clothes, etc. I was to remain with him three years. My first day's work was turning a big heavy stone for him to grind a lot of old, rusty tools on. That night after supper I broke my contract, as I concluded that I knew just as much about the carpenter's trade as I wished to know, and skipped for the country, by moonlight.

I landed up at a Mr. Jacobs' farm twelve miles from town and got a job of work at twelve dollars a month. I didn't remain there long though, as I had a chill every other day regular, and therefore couldn't work much.

I made up my mind then to pull for Saint Louis and hunt mother and sister. I had never heard a word from them since they left. After buying a small satchel to put my clothes in and paying for a ticket to the city, I had only twenty-five cents left and part of that I spent for dinner that day.

I arrived in East Saint Louis about midnight with only ten cents left. I wanted to buy a ginger-cake or something as I was very hungry, but hated to as I needed the dime to pay my way across the river next morning. I wasn't very well posted then, in regard to the ways of getting on in the world, or I would have spent the dime for something to eat, and then beat my way across the river.

CHAPTER TWO

A MOONLIGHT DRIVE

by Andy Adams

Cowboy handling cattle, author unknown, 1902.

The two herds were held together a second night, but after they had grazed a few hours the next morning, the cattle were thrown together, and the work of cutting out ours commenced. With a double outfit of men available, about twenty men were turned into the herd to do the cutting, the remainder holding the main herd and looking after the cut. The morning was cool, every one worked with a vim, and in about two hours the herds were again separated and ready for the final trimming. Campbell did not expect to move out until he could communicate with the head office of the company, and would go up to Fort Laramie for that purpose during the day, hoping to be able to get a message over the military wire. When his outfit had finished retrimming our herd, and we had looked over his cattle for the last time, the two outfits bade each other farewell, and our herd started on its journey.

The unfortunate accident at the ford had depressed our feelings to such an extent that there was an entire absence of hilarity, by the way. This morning the farewell songs generally used in parting with a river which had defied us were omitted. The herd trailed out like an immense serpent, and was guided and controlled by our men as if by mutes. Long before the noon hour, we passed out of sight of Forty Islands, and in the next few days, with the change of scene, the gloom gradually lifted. We were bearing almost due north, and passing through a delightful country. To our left ran a range of mountains, while on the other hand sloped off the apparently limitless plain. The scarcity of water was beginning to be felt, for the streams which had not a source in the mountains on our left had dried up weeks before our arrival. There was a gradual change of air noticeable too, for we were rapidly gaining altitude, the heat of summer being now confined to a few hours at noonday, while the nights were almost too cool for our comfort.

When about three days out from the North Platte, the mountains disappeared on our left, while on the other hand appeared a rugged-looking country, which we knew must be the approaches of the Black Hills. Another day's drive brought us into the main stage road connecting the railroad on the south with the mining camps which nestled somewhere in those rocky hills to our right. The stage road followed the trail some ten or fifteen miles before we parted company with it on a dry fork of the Big Cheyenne River. There was a road house and stage stand where these two thoroughfares separated, the one to the mining camp of Deadwood, while ours of the Montana cattle trail bore off for the Powder River to the northwest. At this stage stand we learned that some twenty herds had already passed by to the northern ranges, and that after passing the next fork of the Big Cheyenne we should find no water until we struck the Powder River—a stretch of eighty miles. The keeper of the road house, a genial host, informed us that this droughty stretch in our front was something unusual, this being one of the dryest summers that he had experienced since the discovery of gold in the Black Hills.

Here was a new situation to be met, an eighty-mile dry drive; and with our experience of a few months before at Indian Lakes fresh in our memories, we set our house in order for the undertaking before us. It was yet fifteen miles to the next and last water from the stage stand. There were several dry forks of the Cheyenne beyond, but as they had their source in the tablelands of Wyoming, we could not hope for water in their dry bottoms. The situation was serious, with only this encouragement: other herds had crossed this arid belt since the streams had dried up, and our Circle Dots could walk with any herd that ever left Texas. The wisdom of mounting us well for just such an emergency reflected the good cow sense of our employer; and we felt easy in regard to our mounts, though there was not a horse or a man too many. In summing up the situation, Flood said, "We've got this advantage over the Indian Lake drive: there is a good moon, and the days are cool. We'll make twenty-five miles a day covering this stretch, as this herd has never been put to a test yet to see how far they could walk in a day. They'll have to do their sleeping at noon; at least cut it into two shifts, and if we get any sleep we'll have to do the same. Let her come as she will; every day's drive is a day nearer the Blackfoot agency."

We made a dry camp that night on the divide between the road house and the last water, and the next forenoon reached the South Fork of the Big Cheyenne. The water was not even running in it, but there were several long pools, and we held the cattle around them for over an hour, until every hoof had been thoroughly watered. McCann had filled every keg and canteen in advance of the arrival of the herd, and Flood had exercised sufficient caution, in view of what lay before us, to buy an extra keg and a bull's-eye lantern at the road house. After watering, we trailed out some four or five miles and camped for noon, but the herd were allowed to graze forward until they lay down for their noonday rest. As the herd passed opposite the wagon, we cut a fat two-year-old stray heifer and killed her for beef, for the inner man must be fortified for the journey before us. After a two hours' siesta, we threw the herd on the trail and started on our way. The wagon and saddle horses were held in our immediate rear, for there was no telling when or where we would make our next halt of any consequence. We trailed and grazed the herd alternately until near evening, when the wagon was sent on ahead about three miles to get supper, while half the outfit went along to change mounts and catch up horses for those remaining behind with the herd. A half hour before the usual bedding time, the relieved men returned and took the grazing herd, and the others rode in to the wagon for supper and a change of mounts. While we shifted our saddles, we smelled the savory odor of fresh beef frying.

"Listen to that good old beef talking, will you?" said Joe Stallings, as he was bridling his horse. "McCann, I'll take my *carne fresco* a trifle rare to-night, garnished with a sprig of parsley and a wee bit of lemon."

Before we had finished supper, Honeyman had rehooked the mules to the wagon, while the *remuda* was at hand to follow. Before we left the wagon, a full moon was rising on the eastern horizon, and as we were starting out Flood gave us these general directions: "I'm going to take the lead with the cook's lantern, and one of you rear men take the new bull's-eye. We'll throw the herd on the trail; and between the lead and rear light, you swing men want to ride well outside, and you point men want to hold the lead cattle so the rear will never be more than a half a mile behind. I'll admit that this is somewhat of an experiment with me, but I don't see any good reason why she won't work. After the moon gets another hour high we can see a quarter of a mile, and the cattle are so well trail broke they'll never try to scatter. If it works all right, we'll never bed them short of midnight, and that will put us ten miles farther. Let's ride, lads."

By the time the herd was eased back on the trail, our evening camp-fire had been passed, while the cattle led out as if walking on a wager. After the first mile on the trail, the men on the point were compelled to ride in the lead if we were to hold them within the desired half mile. The men on the other side, or the swing, were gradually widening, until the herd must have reached fully a mile in length; yet we swing riders were never out of sight of each other, and it would have been impossible for any cattle to leave the herd unnoticed. In that moonlight the trail was as plain as day, and after an hour, Flood turned his lantern over to one of the point men, and rode back around the herd to the rear. From my position that first night near the middle of the swing, the lanterns both rear and forward being always in sight, I was as much at sea as any one as to the length of the herd, knowing the deceitfulness of distance of campfires and other lights by night. The foreman appealed to me as he rode down the column, to know the length of the herd, but I could give him no more than a simple guess. I could assure him, however, that the cattle had made no effort to drop out and leave the trail. But a short time after he passed me I noticed a horseman galloping up the column on the opposite side of the herd, and knew it must be the foreman. Within a short time, someone in the lead wig-wagged his lantern; it was answered by the light in the rear, and the next minute the old rear song,—

"Ip-e-la-ago, go 'long little doggie,
You 'll make a beef-steer by-and-by,"—

reached us riders in the swing, and we knew the rear guard of cattle was being pushed forward. The distance between the swing men gradually narrowed in our lead, from which we could tell the leaders were being held in, until several times cattle grazed out from the herd, due to the checking in front. At this juncture Flood galloped around the herd a

Cattle crossing the Smoky Hill River at Ellsworth, on the old Santa Fe crossing, by A. Gardner, 1867.

second time, and as he passed us riding along our side, I appealed to him to let them go in front, as it now required constant riding to keep the cattle from leaving the trail to graze. When he passed up the opposite side, I could distinctly hear the men on that flank making a similar appeal, and shortly afterwards the herd loosened out and we struck our old gait for several hours.

Trailing by moonlight was a novelty to all of us, and in the stillness of those splendid July nights we could hear the point men chatting across the lead in front, while well in the rear, the rattling of our heavily loaded wagon and the whistling of the horse wrangler to his charges reached our ears. The swing men were scattered so far apart there was no chance for conversation amongst us, but every once in a while a song would be started, and as it surged up and down the line, every voice, good, bad, and indifferent, joined in. Singing is supposed to have a soothing effect on cattle, though I will vouch for the fact that none of our Circle Dots stopped that night to listen to our vocal efforts. The herd was traveling so nicely that our foreman hardly noticed the passing hours, but along about midnight the singing ceased, and we were nodding in our saddles and wondering if they in the lead were never going to throw off the trail, when a great wig-wagging occurred in front, and presently we overtook The Rebel, holding the lantern and turning the herd out of the trail. It was then after midnight, and within another half hour we had the cattle bedded down within a few hundred yards of the trail. One-hour guards was the order of the night, and as soon as our wagon and saddle horses came up, we stretched ropes and caught out our night horses. These we either tied to the wagon wheels or picketed near at hand, and then we sought our blankets for a few hours' sleep. It was half past three in the morning when our guard was called, and before the hour passed, the first signs of day were visible in the east. But even before our watch had ended, Flood and the last guard came to our relief, and we pushed the sleeping cattle off the bed ground and started them grazing forward.

Cattle will not graze freely in a heavy dew or too early in the morning, and before the sun was high enough to dry the grass, we had put several miles behind us. When the sun was about an hour high, the remainder of the outfit overtook us, and shortly afterward the wagon and saddle horses passed on up the trail, from which it was evident that "breakfast would be served in the dining car ahead," as the traveled Priest aptly put it. After the sun was well up, the cattle grazed freely for several hours; but when we sighted the *remuda* and our commissary some two miles in our lead, Flood ordered the herd lined up for a count. The Rebel was always a reliable counter, and he and the foreman now rode forward and selected the crossing of a dry wash for the counting. On receiving their signal to come on, we allowed the herd to graze slowly forward, but gradually pointed them into an immense "V," and as the point of the herd crossed the dry arroyo, we compelled them to pass in a narrow file between the two counters, when they again spread out fan-like and continued their feeding.

The count confirmed the success of our driving by night, and on its completion all but two men rode to the wagon for breakfast. By the time the morning meal was disposed of, the herd had come up parallel with the wagon but a mile to the westward, and as fast as fresh mounts could be saddled, we rode away in small squads to relieve the herders and to turn the cattle into the trail. It was but a little after eight o'clock in the morning when the herd was again trailing out on the Powder River trail, and we had already put over thirty miles of the dry drive behind us, while so far neither horses nor cattle had been put to any extra exertion. The wagon followed as usual, and for over three hours we held the trail without a break, when sighting a divide in our front, the foreman went back and sent the wagon around the herd with instructions to make the noon camp well up on the divide. We threw the herd off the trail, within a mile of this stopping place, and allowed them to graze, while two thirds of the outfit galloped away to the wagon.

We allowed the cattle to lie down and rest to their complete satisfaction until the middle of the afternoon; meanwhile all hands, with the exception of two men on herd, also lay down and slept in the shade of the wagon. When the cattle had had several hours' sleep, the want of water made them restless, and they began to rise and graze away. Then all hands were aroused and we threw them upon the trail. The heat of the day was already over, and until the twilight of the evening, we trailed a three-mile clip, and again threw the herd off to graze. By our traveling and grazing gaits, we could form an approximate idea as to the distance we had covered, and the consensus of opinion of all was that we had already killed over half the distance. The herd was beginning to show the want of water by evening, but amongst our saddle horses the lack of water was more noticeable, as a horse subsisting on grass alone weakens easily; and riding them made them all the more gaunt. When we caught up our mounts that evening, we had used eight horses to the man since we had left the South Fork, and another one would be required at midnight, or whenever we halted.

We made our drive the second night with more confidence than the one before, but there were times when the train of cattle must have been nearly two miles in length, yet there was never a halt as long as the man with the lead light could see the one in the rear. We bedded the herd about midnight; and at the first break of day, the fourth guard with the foreman joined us on our watch and we started the cattle again. There was a light dew the second night, and the cattle, hungered by their night walk, went to grazing at once on the damp grass, which would allay their thirst slightly. We allowed them to scatter over several thousand acres, for we were anxious to graze them well before the sun absorbed the moisture, but at the same time every step they took was one less to the coveted Powder River.

When we had grazed the herd forward several miles, and the sun was nearly an hour high, the wagon failed to come up, which caused our foreman some slight uneasiness. Nearly another hour passed, and still the wagon did not come up nor did the outfit put in an appearance. Soon afterwards, however, Moss Strayhorn overtook us, and reported that over forty of our saddle horses were missing, while the work mules had been overtaken nearly five miles back on the trail. On account of my ability as a trailer, Flood at once dispatched me to assist Honeyman in recovering the missing horses, instructing someone else to take the *remuda*, and the wagon and horses to follow up the herd. By the time I arrived, most of the boys at camp had secured a change of horses, and I caught up my *grulla*, that I was saving for the last hard ride, for the horse hunt which confronted us. McCann, having no fire built, gave Honeyman and myself an impromptu breakfast and two canteens of water; but before we let the wagon get away, we rustled a couple of cans of tomatoes and buried them in a cache near the camp-ground, where we would have no trouble in finding them on our return. As the wagon pulled out, we mounted our horses and rode back down the trail.

Billy Honeyman understood horses, and at once volunteered the belief that we would have a long ride overtaking the missing saddle stock. The absent horses, he said, were principally the ones which had been under saddle the day before, and as we both knew, a tired, thirsty horse will go miles for water. He recalled, also, that while we were asleep at noon the day before, twenty miles back on the trail, the horses had found quite a patch of wild sorrel plant, and were foolish over leaving it. Both of us being satisfied that this would hold them for several hours at least, we struck a free gait for it. After we passed the point where the mules had been overtaken, the trail of the horses was distinct enough for us to follow in an easy canter. We saw frequent signs that they left the trail, no doubt to graze, but only for short distances, when they would enter it again, and keep it for miles. Shortly before noon, as we gained the divide above our noon camp of the day before, there about two miles distant we saw our missing horses, feeding over an alkali flat on which grew wild sorrel and other species of sour plants. We rounded them up, and finding none missing, we first secured a change of mounts. The only two horses of my mount in this portion of the *remuda* had both been under saddle the afternoon and night before, and were as gaunt as rails, and Honeyman had one unused horse of his mount in the band. So when, taking down our ropes, we halted the horses and began riding slowly around them, forcing them into a compact body, I had my eye on a brown horse of Flood's that had not had a saddle on in a week, and told Billy to fasten to him if he got a chance. This was in violation of all custom, but if the foreman kicked, I had a good excuse to offer.

Honeyman was left-handed and threw a rope splendidly; and as we circled around the horses on opposite sides, on a signal from him we whirled our lariats and made casts simultaneously. The wrangler fastened to the brown I wanted, and my loop settled around the neck of his unridden horse. As the band broke away from our swinging ropes, a number of them ran afoul of my rope; but I gave the rowel to my *grulla*, and we shook them off. When I returned to Honeyman, and we had exchanged horses and were shifting our saddles, I complimented him on the long throw he had made in catching the brown, and incidentally mentioned that I had read of vaqueros in California who used a sixty-five foot lariat. "Hell," said Billy, in ridicule of the idea, "there wasn't a man ever born who could throw a sixty-five foot rope its full length—without he threw it down a well."

The sun was straight overhead when we started back to overtake the herd. We struck into a little better than a five-mile gait on the return trip, and about two o'clock sighted a band of saddle horses and a wagon camped perhaps a mile forward and to the side of the trail. On coming near enough, we saw at a glance it was a cow outfit, and after driving our loose horses a good push beyond their camp, turned and rode back to their wagon.

"We'll give them a chance to ask us to eat," said Billy to me, "and if they don't, why, they'll miss a hell of a good chance to entertain hungry men."

But the foreman with the stranger wagon proved to be a Bee County Texan, and our doubts did him an injustice, for, although dinner was over, he invited us to dismount and ordered his cook to set out something to eat. They had met our wagon, and McCann had insisted on their taking a quarter of our beef, so we fared well. The outfit was from a ranch near Miles City, Montana, and were going down to receive a herd of cattle at Cheyenne, Wyoming. The cattle had been bought at Ogalalla for delivery at the former point, and this wagon was going down with their ranch outfit to take the herd on its arrival. They had brought along about seventy-five saddle horses from the ranch, though in buying the herd they had taken its *remuda* of over a hundred saddle horses. The foreman informed us that they had met our cattle about the middle of the forenoon, nearly twenty-five miles out from Powder River. After we had satisfied the inner man, we lost no time getting off, as we could see a long ride ahead of us; but we had occasion as we rode away to go through their *remuda* to cut out a few of our horses which had mixed, and I found I knew over a dozen of their horses by the ranch brands, while Honeyman also recognized quite a few. Though we felt a pride in our mounts, we had to admit that theirs were better; for the effect of climate had transformed horses that we had once ridden on ranches in southern Texas. It does seem incredible, but it is a fact nevertheless, that a horse, having reached the years of maturity in a southern climate, will grow half a hand taller and carry two hundred pounds more flesh, when he has undergone the rigors of several northern winters.

We halted at our night camp to change horses and to unearth our cached tomatoes, and again set out. By then it was so late in the day that the sun had lost its force, and on this last leg in overtaking the herd we increased our gait steadily until the sun was scarcely an hour high, and yet we never sighted a dust-cloud in our front. About sundown we called a few minutes' halt, and after eating our tomatoes and drinking the last of our water, again pushed on. Twilight had faded into dusk before we reached a divide which we had had in sight for several hours, and which we had hoped to gain in time to sight the timber on Powder River before dark. But as we put mile after mile behind us, that divide seemed to move away like a mirage, and the evening star had been shining for an hour before we finally reached it, and sighted, instead of Powder's timber, the campfire of our outfit about five miles ahead. We fired several shots on seeing the light, in the hope that they might hear us in camp and wait; otherwise we knew they would start the herd with the rising of the moon.

When we finally reached camp, about nine o'clock at night, everything was in readiness to start, the moon having risen sufficiently. Our shooting, however, had been heard, and horses for a change were tied to the wagon wheels, while the remainder of the *remuda* was under herd in charge of Rod Wheat. The runaways were thrown into the horse herd while we bolted our suppers. Meantime McCann informed us that Flood had ridden that afternoon to the Powder River, in order to get the lay of the land. He had found it to be ten or twelve miles distant from the present camp, and the water in the river barely knee deep to a saddle horse. Beyond it was a fine valley. Before we started, Flood rode in from the herd, and said to Honeyman, "I'm going to send the horses and wagon ahead to-night, and you and McCann want to camp on this side of the river, under the hill and just a few hundred yards below the ford. Throw your saddle horses across the river, and build a fire before you go to sleep, so we will have a beacon light to pilot us in, in case the cattle break into a run on scenting the water. The herd will get in a little after midnight, and after crossing, we'll turn her loose just for luck."

It did me good to hear the foreman say the herd was to be turned loose, for I had been in the saddle since three that morning, had ridden over eighty miles, and had now ten more in sight, while Honeyman would complete the day with over a hundred to his credit. We let the *remuda* take the lead in pulling out, so that the wagon mules could be spurred to their utmost in keeping up with the loose horses. Once they were clear of the herd, we let the cattle into the trail. They had refused to bed down, for they were uneasy with thirst, but the cool weather had saved them any serious suffering. We all felt gala as the herd strung out on the trail. Before we halted again there would be water for our dumb brutes and rest for ourselves. There was lots of singing that night. "There's One more River to Cross," and "Roll, Powder, Roll," were wafted out on the night air to the coyotes that howled on our flanks, or to the prairie dogs as they peeped from their burrows at this weird caravan of the night, and the lights which flickered in our front and rear must have been real Jack-o'-lanterns or Will-o'-the-wisps to these occupants of the plain. Before we had covered half the distance, the herd was strung out over two miles, and as Flood rode back to the rear every half hour or so, he showed no inclination to check the lead and give the sore-footed rear guard a chance to close up the column; but about an hour before midnight we saw a light low down in our front, which gradually increased until the treetops were distinctly visible, and we knew that our wagon had reached the river. On sighting this beacon, the long yell went up and down the column, and the herd walked as only long-legged, thirsty Texas cattle can walk when they scent water. Flood called all the swing men to the rear, and we threw out a half-circle skirmish line covering a mile in width, so far back that only an occasional glimmer of the lead light could be seen. The trail struck the Powder on an angle, and when within a mile of the river, the swing cattle left the deep-trodden paths and started for the nearest water.

The left flank of our skirmish line encountered the cattle as they reached the river, and prevented them from drifting up the stream. The point men abandoned the leaders when within a few hundred yards of the river. Then the rear guard of cripples and sore-footed cattle came up, and the two flanks of horsemen pushed them all across the river until they met, when we turned and galloped into camp, making the night hideous with our yelling. The longest dry drive of the trip had been successfully made, and we all felt jubilant. We stripped bridles and saddles from our tired horses, and unrolling our beds, were soon lost in well-earned sleep.

The stars may have twinkled overhead, and sundry voices of the night may have whispered to us as we lay down to sleep, but we were too tired for poetry or sentiment that night.

CHAPTER THREE
CATTLE DETECTIVE
Tom Horn

"The Cow Boy" by John C. H. Grabill, 1887.

Early in April of 1887, some of the boys came down from the Pleasant Valley, where there was a big rustler war going on and the rustlers were getting the best of the game. I was tired of the mine and willing to go, and so away we went. Things were in a pretty bad condition. It was war to the knife between cowboys and rustlers, and there was a battle every time the two outfits ran together. A great many men were killed in the war. Old man Blevins and his three sons, three of the Grahams, a Bill Jacobs, Jim Payne, Al Rose, John Tewkesbury, Stolt, Scott, and a man named "Big Jeff" were hung on the Apache and Gila County line. Others were killed, but I do not remember their names now. I was the mediator, and was deputy sheriff under Bucky O'Neil, of Yavapai County, under Commodore Owens, of Apache County, and Glenn Reynolds, of Gila County. I was still a deputy for Reynolds a year later when he was killed by the Apache Kid, in 1888.

After this war in the Pleasant Valley I again went back to my mine and went to work, but it was too slow, and I could not stay at it. I was just getting ready to go to Mexico and was going down to clean out the spring at the mine one evening. I turned my saddle horse loose and let him graze up the *cañon*. After I got the spring cleaned out, I went up the *cañon* to find my horse and I saw a moccasin track covering the trail made by the rope my horse was dragging. That meant to go back, but I did not go back. I cut up the side of the mountain and found the trail where my horse had gone out. It ran into the trail of several more horses, and they were all headed south. I went down to the ranch, got another horse and rode over to the Agency, about twenty miles, to get an Indian or two to go with me to see what I could learn about this bunch of Indians.

I got to the Agency about two o'clock in the morning and found that there had been an outbreak and mutiny among Sieber's police. It was like this: Sieber had raised a young Indian he always called "the Kid," and now known as the "Apache Kid." This kid was the son of old Chief Toga-de-chuz, a San Carlos Apache. At a big dance on the Gila at old Toga-de-chuz's camp everybody got drunk and when morning came old Toga was found dead from a knife thrust. An old hunter belonging to another tribe of Indians and called "Rip" was accused of doing the job, but from what Sieber could learn, as he afterwards told me, everybody was too drunk to know how the thing did happen. The wound was given in a very skillful manner and as it split open old Toga's heart it was supposed to be given by one who knew where the heart lay.

Toga and old Rip had had a row over a girl about forty years before (they were both about sixty at this time), and Toga had gotten the best of the row and the girl to boot. Some say that an Indian will forget and forgive the same as a white man. I say no. Here had elapsed forty years between the row and the time old Toga was killed.

Rip had not turned his horse loose in the evening before the killing, so it was supposed he had come there with express intention of killing old Toga.

Anyway the Kid was the oldest son of Toga-de-chuz and he must revenge the death of his father. He must, according to all Indian laws and customs, kill old Rip. Sieber knew this and cautioned the Kid about doing anything to old Rip. The Kid never said a word to Sieber as to what he would do. The Kid was first sergeant of the Agency scouts. The Interior Department had given the Agency over to the military and there were no more police, but scouts instead.

Shortly after this killing, Sieber and Captain Pierce, the agent, went up to Camp Apache to see about the distribution of some annuities to the Indians there, and the Kid, as first sergeant of the scouts, was left in charge of the peace of the Agency.

No sooner did Sieber and Captain Pierce get started than the Kid took five of his men and went over on the Aravaipo, where old Rip lived, and shot him. That evened up their account, and the Kid went back to where his band was living up above the Agency. Sieber heard of this and he and Pierce immediately started to San Carlos.

When they got there, they found no one in command of the scouts. Sieber sent word up to the camp where the Kid's people lived to tell the Kid to come down. This he did, escorted by the whole band of bucks.

Sieber, when they drew up in front of his tent, went out and spoke to the Kid and told him to get off his horse, and this the Kid did. Sieber then told him to take the arms of the other four or five men who had government rifles. This also the Kid did. He took their guns and belts and then Sieber told him to take off his own belt and put down his gun and take the other deserters and go to the guardhouse.

Some of the bucks with the Kid (those who were not soldiers) said to the Kid to fight, and in a second they were at it—eleven bucks against Sieber alone. It did not make any particular difference to Sieber about being outnumbered. His rifle was in his tent. He jumped back and got it, and at the first shot he killed one Indian. All the others fired at him as he came to the door of his tent, but only one bullet struck him; that hit him on the shin and shattered his leg all to pieces. He fell, and the Indian ran away.

This was what Sieber told me when I got to the Agency. And then I knew it was the Kid who had my horse and outfit. Soldiers were already on his trail.

From where he had stolen my horse, he and his band crossed over the mountain to the Table Mountain district, and there stole a lot of Bill Atchley's saddle horses. A few miles further on they killed Bill Dihl, then headed on up through the San Pedro country, turned down the Sonoita River, and there they killed Mike Grace; then they were turned back north again by some of the cavalry that was after them.

They struck back north, and Lieutenant Johnson got after them about Pontaw, overtook them in the Rincon Mountains, and had a fight, killing a couple of them, and put all the rest of them afoot. My horse was captured unwounded, and as the soldiers knew him, he was taken to the San Pedro and left there; they sent word to me, and eventually I got him, though he was pretty badly used up.

That was the way the Kid came to break out. He went back to the Reservation, and later on he surrendered. He was tried for desertion, and given a long time by the federal courts, but was pardoned by President Cleveland, after having served a short term.

During the time the Kid and his associates were hiding around on the Reservation, previous to his first arrest, he and his men had killed a freighter, or he may have been only a whisky peddler. Anyway, he was killed twelve miles above San Carlos, on the San Carlos River, by the Kid's outfit, and when the Kid returned to the Agency after he had done his short term and had been pardoned by the President, he was rearrested by the civil authorities of Gila County, Arizona, to be tried for the killing of this man at the Twelve Mile Pole.

This was in the fall of 1888. I was deputy sheriff of Gila County at that time, and as it was a new county, Reynolds was the first sheriff. I was to be the interpreter at the Kid's trial, but on July 4, 1888, I had won the prize at the Globe for tying down a steer, and there was

a county rivalry among the cowboys all over the Territory as to who was the quickest man at that business. One Charley Meadows (whose father and brother were before mentioned as being killed by the Cibicus on their raid) was making a big talk that he could beat me tying at the Territorial Fair, at Phoenix. Our boys concluded I must go to the fair and make a trial for the Territorial prize, and take out Meadows. I had known Meadows for years, and I thought I could beat him, and so did my friends.

The fair came off at the same time as did court in our new county, and since I could not very well be at both places, and, as they said, could not miss the fair, I was not at the trial.

While I was at Phoenix, the trial came off and several of the Indians told about the killing. There were six on trial, and they were all sentenced to the penitentiary at Yuma, Arizona, for life. Reynolds and "Hunky Dory" Holmes started to take them to Yuma. There were the six Indians and a Mexican sent up for one year, for horse stealing. The Indians had their hands coupled together, so that there were three in each of the two bunches.

Where the stage road from Globe to Casa Grande (the railroad station on the Southern Pacific Railroad) crosses the Gila river there is a very steep sand wash, up which the stage road winds. Going up this, Reynolds took his prisoners out and they were all walking behind the stage. The Mexican was handcuffed and inside the stage. Holmes got ahead of Reynolds some little distance. Holmes had three Indians and Reynolds three.

Just as Holmes turned a short bend in the road and got behind a point of rocks and out of sight of Reynolds, at a given signal, each bunch of prisoners turned on their guard and grappled with him. Holmes was soon down and they killed him. The three that had tackled Reynolds were not doing so well, but the ones that had killed

Holmes got his rifle and pistol and went to the aid of the ones grappling Reynolds. These three were holding his arms so he could not get his gun. The ones that came up killed him, took his keys, unlocked the cuffs, and they were free.

Gene Livingston was driving the stage, and he looked around the side of the stage to see what the shooting was about. One of the desperadoes took a shot at him, striking him over the eye, and down he came. The Kid and his men then took the stage horses and tried to ride them, but there was only one of the four that they could ride.

The Kid remained an outlaw after that, till he died a couple of years ago of consumption. The Mexican, after the Kid and his men left the stage (they had taken off his handcuffs), struck out for Florence and notified the authorities. The driver was only stunned by the shot over the eye and is a resident and business man of Globe.

Had I not been urged to go to the fair at Phoenix, this would never have happened, as the Kid and his comrades just walked along and put up the job in their own language, which no one there could understand but themselves. Had I not gone to the fair, I would have been with Reynolds and could have understood what they said and it would never have happened. I won the prize roping at the fair, but it was at a very heavy cost.

In the winter I again went home, and in the following spring I went to work on my mine. Worked along pretty steady on it for a year, and in 1890 we sold it to a party of New Yorkers. We got $8,000 for it.

We were negotiating for this sale, and at the same time the Pinkerton National Detective Agency at Denver, Colorado, was writing to me to get me to come to Denver and to go to work for them. I thought it would be a good thing to do, and as soon as all the arrangements for the sale of the mine were made, I came to Denver and was initiated into the mysteries of the Pinkerton institution.

My work for them was not the kind that exactly suited my disposition; too tame for me. There were a good many instructions and a good deal of talk given the operative regarding the things to do and the things that had been done.

James McParland, the superintendent, asked me what I would do if I were put on a train robbery case. I told him if I had a good man with me I could catch up to them.

Well, on the last night of August, that year, at about midnight, a train was robbed on the Denver & Rio Grande Railway, between Cotopaxi and Texas Creek. I was sent out there, and was told that C.W. Shores would be along in a day or so. He came on time and asked me how I was getting on. I told him I had struck the trail, but there were so many men scouring the country that I, myself, was being held up all the time; that I had been arrested twice in two days and taken in to Salida to be identified!

Eventually all the sheriff's posses quit, and then Mr. W. A. Pinkerton and Mr. McParland told Shores and me to go at 'em. We took up the trail where I had left it several days before and we never left it till we got the robbers.

They had crossed the Sangre de Cristo range, come down by the Villa Grove iron mines, and crossed back to the east side of the Sangre de Cristos at Mosca Pass, then on down through the Huerfano Cañon, out by Cucharas, thence down east of Trinidad. They had dropped into Clayton, N.M., and got into a shooting scrape there in a gin mill. They then turned east again toward the "Neutral Strip" and close to Beaver City, then across into the "Pan Handle" by a place in Texas called Ochiltree, the county seat of Ochiltree County. They then headed toward the Indian Territory, and crossed into it below Canadian City. They then swung in on the head of the Washita River in the Territory, and kept down this river for a long distance.

We finally saw that we were getting close to them, as we got in the neighborhood of Paul's Valley. At Washita station we located one of them in the house of a man by the name of Wolfe. The robber's name was Burt Curtis. Shores took this one and came on back to Denver, leaving me to get the other one if ever he came back to Wolfe's.

After several days of waiting on my part, he did come back, and as he came riding up to the house I stepped out and told him someone had come! He was "Peg Leg" Watson, and considered by everyone in Colorado as a very desperate character. I had no trouble with him.

We had an idea that Joe McCoy, also, was in the robbery, but "Peg" said he was not, and gave me information enough so that I located him. He was wanted very badly by the sheriff of Fremont County, Colorado, for a murder scrape. He and his father had been tried previous to this for murder, had been found guilty, and were remanded to jail to wait sentence, but before Joe was sentenced he had escaped. The old man McCoy got a new trial, and at the new trial was sentenced to eighteen years in the Cañon City, Colorado, penitentiary.

When I captured my man, got to a telegraph station and wired Mr. McParland that I had the notorious "Peg," the superintendent wired back: "Good! Old man McCoy got eighteen years today!" This train had been robbed in order to get money to carry McCoy's case up to the Supreme Court, or rather to pay the attorneys (Macons & Son), who had carried the case up.

Later on I told Mr. McParland that I could locate Joe McCoy, and he communicated with Stewart, the sheriff, who came to Denver and made arrangements for me to go with him and try to get McCoy.

We left Denver on Christmas Eve and went direct to Rifle, from there to Meeker, and on down White River. When we got to where McCoy had been, we learned that he had gone to Ashley, in Utah, for the Christmas festivities. We pushed on over there, reaching the town late at night and could not locate our man. Next morning I learned where he got his meals, and as he went in to get his breakfast, I followed him in and arrested him. He had a big Colt's pistol, but did not shoot me. We took him out by Fort Duchesne, Utah, and caught the D.& R. G. train at Price station.

The judge under whom he had been tried had left the bench when McCoy finally was landed back in jail, and it would have required a new trial before he could be sentenced by another judge; he consented to plead guilty to involuntary manslaughter, and took six years in the Cañon City pen. He was pardoned out in three years, I believe.

Peg Leg Watson and Burt Curtis were tried in the United States court for robbing the United States mails on the highway, and were sentenced for life in the Detroit federal prison. In robbing the train they had first made the fireman break into the mail compartment of the compartment car. They then saw their mistake, and did not even take the amount of a one-cent postage stamp, but went and made the fireman break into the rear compartment, where they found the express matter, and took it. But the authorities proved that it was mail robbery and their sentence was life.

While Pinkerton's is one of the greatest institutions of the kind in existence, I never did like the work, so I left them in 1894.

I then came to Wyoming and went to work for the Swan Land and Cattle Company, since which time everybody else has been more familiar with my life and business than I have been myself.

And I think that since my coming here the yellow journal reporters are better equipped to write my history than am I, myself!

Respectfully,
TOM HORN

* * *

"In Arizona and New Mexico, roping contests used to be held as a kind of annual tournament, in August, to the fair, or else as a special entertainment, often comprising, among other features, horse racing, a bull fight, baile and fiesta. Roping contests are generally held in a large field or enclosure—such as the interior of a race course. Inside this compound is built a small corral, in which are confined wild beef cattle, usually three-year-old steers, just rounded up off the range.

"The contest is a time race, to see who can overtake, lasso, throw and tie hard and fast the feet of a steer in the shortest period. The record was made at Phoenix, Arizona, in 1891. The contestants were, Charlie Meadows, Bill McCann, George Iago, Ramon Barca and Tom Horn, all well-known vaqueros of the Mexican-Arizona border. Tom Horn won the contest. Time, 49 ½ seconds, which I do not think has since been lowered.

"Two parallel lines, about as far apart as the ends of a polo court, were marked by banderoles or guidons. A steer was let out of the corral and driven at a run in a direction at right angles to the lines marked. As the steer crossed the second line, a banderole was dropped, which was the signal for a vaquero to start from the first line, thus giving the beef a running start of 250 yards. The horses used were all large, fleet animals, wonderfully well trained, and swooped for their prey at full speed and by the shortest route, turning without a touch of the rein to follow the steer, often anticipating his turns by a shorter cut. When the vaquero got within fifty yards of his beef the loop of his riata was swinging in a sharp, crisp circle about his right arm, raised high to his right and rear, and when twenty yards closer, it shot forward, hovered for an instant, and then descended above the horns of its victim, which a moment later would land a somersault. Before the beef could recover his surprise or wind he would have a half hitch about his fore legs, a second about his hind legs, and a third found all four a snug little bunch, hard and fast.

"The rope, of course, is not taken from the head; it is all one rope, the slack being successively used. Sometimes the vaqueros used foot-roping instead of head. It requires more skill and is practiced more by the Mexicans, who think it is a good method with large-horned cattle while in herd, where heads are so little separated that a lasso would fall on horns not wanted. In foot-roping the noose is thrown lower and a bit in front of the beef, so that at his next step he will put his foot into the noose before it strikes the ground. If the noose falls too quickly for this, it is jerked sharply upward just as the foot is raised above it.

"I have seen men so skillful at this that they would bet even money on roping an animal on a single throw, naming the foot that they would secure, as right hind, left fore, and so forth. As regards the lash end of the riata, two methods in this contest were also used. In the 'Texas style' the lash of the riata is made hard and fast to the horn of the saddle. The instant the rope 'holds,' a pony who understands his work plants his fore feet forward and checks suddenly, giving the steer a header. His rider dismounts quickly, runs to the beef, which the pony keeps down by holding the rope taut.

"As soon as the vaquero faces the pony and grasps the rope near the beef, the pony moves forward, and with the slack of the rope the beef is secured. While the beef is plunging or wheeling on the rope the pony is careful to keep his head toward the beef, or, as the sailor would say, he goes 'bow on.'

"The Texas method is best adapted to loose ground, where it is much easier on the vaquero, but it is utterly unsuited for mountain work or steep hillsides, as the pony would lose his footing and land up in the bottom of a *cañon*.

"For such country, the California style is used. Here the lash is not made fast; a few frapping turns are made about the horn, and the rider uses his weight and a checking of the pony to throw the beef. When he dismounts, he carries the lash end forward, keeping it taut, toward the beef, taking up the slack and coils it as he goes, and with it secures the beef. The pony is free after the steer is thrown. It is the more rapid method. Tom Horn used it in the contest won, when he made his record. With it the vaquero has free use of his riata for securing the beef. But it is a hard method, and plainsmen prefer letting Mr. Bronco take the brunt of it.

"Tom Horn is well known all along the border. He served as government guide, packer, scout and as chief of Indian scouts, which latter position he held with Captain Crawford at the time the Mexicans killed him in the Sierra Madre Mountains. He is the hero referred to in the story of 'The Killing of the Captain,' by John Heard, Sr., published some months ago in the *Cosmopolitan* Magazine." —Philadelphia *Times*, 1895

CHAPTER FOUR

SOME PRANK

Bob Kennon

"Aiding a Comrade" by Frederick Remingston, 1890.

I was repping for the 79 at the Big State wagon in the Judith Basin when Charlie Russell was a night-hawk. He had held this same job for eleven years. Pete Vann, Bill Skelton, and Teddy Blue Abbott were also there. In later years Vann and Skelton became well-to-do cattlemen in the Geyser country, and Abbott ran cattle below Fort Maginnis.

We had camped on a high divide west of Judith River, about fifteen miles from the river, where there were a number of big springs. Charlie

Russell was as lousy as a pet coon. Pete Vann and Bill Skelton told him to pull off all his clothes and lay them on some anthills nearby.

"Will that take care of the situation?" asked Charlie.

"Yes, the ants will eat all the lice," Bill Skelton answered.

Charlie pondered over this a second or two, then began undressing, putting his clothes on the anthills. The first thing he pulled off was his hat, then his coat and shirt, then off went his pants, lastly his boots. The ants sure had a feast and devoured all the lice. Bill Skelton and Pete Vann walked down to the roundup wagon, bringing back some cottonwood sticks and boards. They drove the stakes into the ground, tied the boards to the sticks with some rawhide strings, took a piece of charcoal from the fire, and printed this sign:

LOUSE CREEK BENCH

This bench is known by that name to this day.

Shortly after I became acquainted with Charlie, he quit riding for a living. Ma Nature seemed to have it planned that he was to make his big pile with his brushes and palette.

He left his mark of friendship and the touch of his genius in many places, and of course in the saloons all over the range country. Every little cow town had his wonderful buffalo, his Indians, his bears, and the pictures of us cowpokes. Dozens of times we found these pictures which he had given to his old friends to decorate their homes and their saloons. Almost everyone knew Charlie, and he visited a lot during the active times of the year and when the weather was good. You could usually locate him every summer at some of his old stomping grounds. The roping and cutting range, the branding corral, and the chuck wagon—these were the things he painted in winter at home in his studio, but in the summer he liked to visit around and take back again these fresh memory pictures of all he loved.

I'll never forget the night I first met Charlie. It happened in Lewistown, and as well as I remember it was in 1897. It seems to me this was the year we had so many good times in Lewistown, when we would come in for a fight with those gold miners from Gilt Edge. I'll certainly always remember that this was the year I met Charlie, and the night when all the drinking went on at the bar next to the stage station, a plenty popular bar for fellows who waited for the usually late stage.

We cowboys came in from Kendall and at this time we were flush with money and with spare time to enjoy ourselves. It was late summer and just before fall roundup. We were itching to try our luck at a few games and have a few drinks before the fellows from Gilt Edge would get into town. There were some among us who would never rest until they could beat up some of these cooty miners, who were due in town this Saturday night. They had been paid off, and were anxious for some poker and whiskey.

Charlie was a great lover of animals, especially the wild ones, so we did a lot of trapping that night over the bar. Looking back to that night, he seemed no different from the rest of us, for he was jolly and full of the devil. He was dressed just like other riders except for that old red sash he always wore. He asked repeatedly how this or that range was, who had sold out their spreads, how the water and grass were, and all those things a range man's always interested in. I'm sure that, though we all liked his pictures, he hadn't the faintest idea of their worth, nor did we appreciate the genius who sat that night laughing and exchanging stories of the Judith and the Musselshell roundups with us.

It was very hot inside, so Charlie and I strolled outside. He pointed up the road and remarked that the dust being stirred up must be the stage coming in. But he was wrong, for it was a buck-board coming in at a good trot. As the vehicle pulled to a stop, we recognized the driver as a rancher who lived not very far from town. He was a good fellow, but had a reputation for getting drunk and staying on a spree for weeks at a time when he got to town. Tonight, though, he refused to be drawn inside the saloon and declared he had come in to meet a friend who was due on the stage from Great Falls.

His name was Hugh McIver and it was whispered around by the hangers-on at the bar that he was waiting for a lady whom he had never met but to whom he had been writing all winter and spring, getting her name and address from one of those "mail-order bride" papers. He was dressed up in a new brown suit, white shirt, green tie, and new hat. His boots were polished to a gloss. He seemed nervous and kept asking about the stage from Great Falls. I was told that he had driven in from his homestead near Lewistown to meet his mail-order bride, whom he had found through that magazine called *Heart and Hand*.

Charlie got quite a kick out of this story, and the homesteader took on a new importance and interest for all of us you may be sure. In spite of his extreme nervousness, we couldn't persuade him to take a drink. I think it might have been all right if it hadn't been for those miners, who now began to arrive in ore wagons, buggies, and on horse-back. As soon as these roughnecks found out that Hughie was waiting for a new bride, he didn't have a chance to stay sober. They dragged him inside bodily and started filling him with whiskey. As soon as he got a little too much, he started giving all his secrets away, and soon he pulled out the lady's picture and these miners were having a regular picnic with him.

Meanwhile, where was the Great Falls to Lewistown stage?

Now perhaps I should tell you that at any season of the year it was a long, hard trip. It had been a wet spring and during the summer we

had had a lot of rain in the early part, so that when we did get the hot weather, the sun baked these deep ruts and chuckholes into a mighty rough road. It took a good twenty-four hours to make the trip with a six-horse team. Of course the teams were changed at the relay stations, which were really ranches or very small cow towns. From Great Falls to Lewistown the stopping places, as I remember, were Belt, Cora Creek, Spion Kop, Old Geyser, Old Stanford, and then, I believe, some ranch halfway between Stanford and Lewistown. Anyway, when travelers got that far, they were pretty sore from the bumps of the road and strangers always asked: "My God, how much farther to Lewistown?"

On this night at the saloon in Lewistown, Charlie tried to talk Hughie into leaving the boys and taking a walk out in the air, but Hughie refused to do so. He showed Charlie and me the lady's picture, though it was now much the worse for the handling and grabbing of the miners, who were bent on pestering the bridegroom. After looking at the photo, which had been done in St. Jo in big-city style, we could see that the lady was certainly a "good looker," to quote Charlie. We both had our doubts, though, as to whether this was the girl Hughie would actually get. This had happened before and it wasn't the first time that a lady sent some beauty's picture instead of her own.

This one was dark haired, with flashing white teeth and large, dark eyes which gazed somewhat boldly at us. "A very flashy sort of gal"—that was what we all agreed. She was dressed fit to kill in white flounces and laces and ribbons, which was the fashion of city ladies at this time. Upon her curls was perched a big white hat, and she carried an umbrella—I think they called it a parasol.

On the back of the photo, Hughie told us, were the full instructions as to how she was to be met at Lewistown and they stated she would be wearing this same outfit and carrying in the other hand a bird cage with her pet canary in it. We later had reason to recall this parasol and bird-cage arrangement.

Now the part about meeting her made Charlie laugh, as he could see that this girl thought she might get lost or the crowd would be so large that Hughie would have a time finding her. We decided that it was time to do something drastic before this lady arrived, for the least we could do would be to see that she was given a decent reception, no matter how things turned out afterward for Hughie. Charlie and the bartender cooked up a plan, and after everyone had a round of drinks the bar was closed and we all went outside to cool off and wait for the stage. There was less objection to this arrangement than we feared, and we hoped we could sober Hughie up out there. To tell the truth, I was for taking him over to the hotel where I had gotten a room earlier in the day and putting him to bed, but Charlie was against this and someone went out promising to get back with some black coffee. Then Charlie spied the water trough where we tended the horses and stage teams and declared that a dip in this cold spring water would be just the thing, but we had to act quick for the stage was due any time. We had Hughie between us, and he refused to even take a drink of the water, though we set a good example by drinking freely of it as it trickled down into the trough. At a sign from Charlie, we gave him a good push and he sprawled into the trough, choking and blubbering.

If we had not gotten him out when we did, he would surely have drowned. We tried to dry him off, but it was so hot this didn't take much effort. Lord, was he mad! It was getting dark by now and all of us went into the stage station and left him outside raving. Charlie said he felt a sort of kinship with anyone coming from Missouri and he was going to see that this lady was treated well.

At last a yell went up as the stage was coming in, with great clouds of dust whirling along the horizon. We rushed out and could hear the rumble of the vehicle and the rattle of the harness on the six-horse team.

Lanterns were brought out and hung up, as was the custom when the passengers were to get out. Of course there was so much pushing and so much chatter and noise that Charlie and I were left way back in the crowd. We craned our necks and pushed too, so we at least could see that a man was helping a lady down. She had on light clothes, and sure enough, Hughie was being called up front. He was there and you must know that he was beyond any sensible conversation.

Soon everyone was going into the station and here we saw that she was indeed the same gal as in the photo. I must state that a lot of fellows lost their bets, as some had bet for sure that she would not show up at all and some others that it would be a different gal. Though it was the same girl, she didn't look as fresh as her picture, for her dress was wrinkled and she seemed wilted all over. She had no hat nor parasol, and indeed no bird cage.

She saw Charlie and rushed to meet him and cuddled in his arms. She kissed him smack on the lips and knocked his Stetson off into the dust. The crowd hooted and hollered, and as Charlie tried to free himself from this unwanted situation, here came the worst-looking spectacle it has been my lot to behold. There stood Hughie, wet and very angry as he clutched the photo. He was pushed forward and introduced to the girl, but she seemed to think it was some joke and still clung to Charlie's arm. Hughie refused to claim her and demanded to see the bird cage, the hat, and the parasol. He seemed to think that he had been cheated. He was just sobering up and at that unhappy stage which makes a man really mean. It took some talking to convince both of them.

Charlie told some bystanders that she should be taken over to Ma Murphy's, who kept a respectable boarding house, and we promised her that we would see what could be done with Hughie when he became more sober. She was a swell-looking girl and no shrinking violet, but now she seemed to have a crush on Charlie and would have traded in Hughie for sure, but we told her Charlie was a married man.

The stage driver even tried to explain to Hughie that he didn't let her bring the bird cage and that it was still up in Great Falls, and that she had nearly been left behind at the halfway station near Lewistown and there she had left her hat and parasol in the rush.

Hughie finally sobered up and came to his senses, and he and his mail-order bride were married by a preacher in Ma Murphy's parlor. Often in later years Charlie would ask me how Hughie's bargain turned out. Her name was Dolly and she was known for miles around, as she bought herself a fancy top buggy and a team of matched bays which she named Granger and Rowdy. They were put up at the livery barn many times when I was there in Lewistown, and many would have paid her a top price for that fine team.

For many years Charlie's path and mine crossed often, but I didn't have the pleasure of meeting his wife until we attended the big Calgary Stampede. I could see then why he had taken up a different life from his earlier and wilder cowboy days, for she was a fine little lady. She was not only pretty, but she had wit and sparkle, often crossing us both in a good argument.

One day Charlie and I were sitting along the bank of the Missouri River where the Milwaukee Railroad depot now stands in Great Falls. As we carried on a lazy sort of general conversation, Charlie picked up a handful of adobe with his left hand and from this he fashioned a perfect image of a bear. He modeled this without even seeming to be looking at what he was doing, and when it was finished he handed it to me. I couldn't help but wonder at such genius, and I wish now I had kept it.

Another time, Charlie and I were at a cigar store, one of his favorite hangouts, next door to the Mint Saloon. Late in the afternoon his wife, Nancy, drove down in their one-horse buggy to take him home. She was sitting in the buggy, near the curb, looking at a fellow standing on the edge of the sidewalk. He had all sorts of tobacco tags on his hat. Charlie drew a picture of this character. In about a week I saw him again and he handed me this picture. It was a perfect likeness. I thanked him, and put the picture in my vest pocket, little knowing how very valuable that sketch would become as time passed. I suppose the picture just wore out there in my pocket.

Sid Willis, owner of the famous Mint Saloon in Great Falls, and Charlie were very close friends. For years the walls of the Mint were lined on either side with large Russell paintings, many of them gifts to Sid from his artist friend, many of them to pay for drinks for other friends. People from all over the United States, as well as foreign lands, paid visits to the Mint to view these paintings. Actually this place was more like an art gallery than a saloon, and here, too, were many of Charlie's finest models done in wax.

Sid was acquainted with many famous people. He and Jaycox, the Milner Livestock Company range boss, went to Texas from Arkansas on horseback. They then decided to come north with a Texas trail herd, the N Bar N outfit. Jaycox secured a job with the Milner Livestock Company, and Sid stayed on with the N Bar N, both of Glasgow, Montana. Later on he became a United States marshal, holding this job for many years. Sid passed away in the early fifties, leaving a void in the friendship of many years which cannot be easily filled. He never ceased grieving for Charlie, who had passed on many years earlier.

Charlie had come back from the Mayo Clinic and was pretty weak. He had suffered a long time from sciatic rheumatism, and now, as he said, his "old pump was givin' out." Before he died on October 24, 1926, he told his wife he wanted to be carried to the cemetery behind horses. Horse-drawn hearses had gone out of style by then and they had to search a long time before they found one in Cascade that had been stored away for years. But his wife saw that his wish was carried out.

As I stood there with the rest of Charlie's friends—which numbered into the hundreds—and watched his riderless horse and the old hearse carry his mortal remains to the cemetery, I felt a sadness that, like many another cowman's, was too deep to be put into any language. He had indeed joined the old trail riders "On the Trail."

PART TWO

COWBOY CHRONICLERS

CHAPTER FIVE

THE COWBOY

Emerson Hough

"A Cowboy on Horseback" by author unknown, 1898-1905.

The great west, vast and rude, brought forth men also vast and rude. We pass today over parts of that matchless region, and we see the red hills and ragged mountain-fronts cut and crushed into huge indefinite shapes, to which even a small imagination may give a human or more than human form. It would almost seem that the same great hand which chiseled out these monumental forms had also laid its fingers upon the people of this region and fashioned them rude and ironlike, in harmony with the stern faces set about them.

Of all the babes of that primeval mother, the West, the cowboy was perhaps her dearest because he was her last. Some of her children lived for centuries; this one for not a triple decade before he began to be old. What was really the life of this child of the wild region of America, and what were the conditions of the experience that bore him, can never be fully known by those who have not seen the West with wide eyes—for the cowboy was simply a part of the West. He who does not understand the one can never understand the other.

If we care truly to see the cowboy as he was and seek to give our wish the dignity of a real purpose, we should study him in connection with his surroundings and in relation to his work. Then we shall see him not as a curiosity but as a product—not as an eccentric driver of horned cattle but as a man suited to his times.

Large tracts of that domain where once the cowboy reigned supreme have been turned into farms by the irrigator's ditch or by the dry-farmer's plan. The farmer in overalls is in many instances his own stockman today. On the ranges of Arizona, Wyoming, and Texas and parts of Nevada we may find the cowboy, it is true, even today: but he is no longer the Homeric figure that once dominated the plains. In what we say as to his trade, therefore, or his fashion in the practice of it, we speak in terms of thirty or forty years ago, when wire was unknown, when the round-up still was necessary, and the cowboy's life was indeed that of the open.

By the costume we may often know the man. The cowboy's costume was harmonious with its surroundings. It was planned upon lines of such stern utility as to leave no possible thing which we may call dispensable. The typical cowboy costume could hardly be said to contain a coat and waistcoat. The heavy woolen shirt, loose and open at the neck, was the common wear at all seasons of the year excepting winter, and one has often seen cowboys in the winter-time engaged in work about the yard or corral of the ranch wearing no other cover for the upper part of the body but one or more of these heavy shirts. If the cowboy wore a coat he would wear it open and loose as much as possible. If he wore a "vest" he would wear it slouchily, hanging open or partly unbuttoned most of the time. There was a reason for this slouchy habit. The cowboy would say that the vest closely buttoned about the body would cause perspiration, so that the wearer would quickly chill upon ceasing exercise. If the wind were blowing keenly when the cowboy dismounted to sit upon the ground for dinner, he would button up his waistcoat and be warm. If it were very cold he would button up his coat also.

The cowboy's boots were of fine leather and fitted tightly, with light narrow soles, extremely small and high heels. Surely a more irrational foot-covering never was invented; yet these tight, peaked cowboy boots had a great significance and may indeed be called the insignia of a calling. There was no prouder soul on earth than the cowboy. He was proud of being a horseman and had a contempt for all human beings who walked. On foot in his tight-toed boots he was lost; but he wished it to be understood that he never was on foot. If we rode beside him and watched his seat in the big cow saddle we found that his high and narrow heels prevented the slipping forward of the foot in the stirrup, into which he jammed his feet nearly full length. If there was a fall, the cowboy's foot never hung in the stirrup. In the corral roping, afoot, his heels anchored him. So he found his little boots not so unserviceable and retained them as a matter of pride. Boots made for the cowboy trade sometimes had fancy tops of bright-colored leather. The Lone Star of Texas was not infrequent in their ornamentation.

The curious pride of the horseman extended also to his gloves. The cowboy was very careful in the selection of his gloves. They were made of the finest buckskin, which could not be injured by wetting. Generally they were tanned white and cut with a deep cuff or gauntlet from which hung a little fringe to flutter in the wind when he rode at full speed on horseback.

The cowboy's hat was one of the typical and striking features of his costumes. It was a heavy, wide, white felt hat with a heavy leather band buckled about it. There has been no other head covering devised so suitable as the Stetson for the uses of the Plains, although high and heavy black hats have in part supplanted it today among stockmen. The boardlike felt was practically indestructible. The brim flapped a little and, in time, was turned up and perhaps held fast to the crown by a thong. The wearer might sometimes stiffen the brim by passing a thong through a series of holes pierced through the outer edge. He could depend upon his hat in all weathers. In the rain it was an umbrella; in the sun a shield; in the winter he could tie it down about his ears with his handkerchief.

Loosely thrown about the cowboy's shirt collar was a silk kerchief. It was tied in a hard knot in front, and though it could scarcely be said to be devoted to the uses of a neck scarf, yet it was a great comfort to the back of the neck when one was riding in a hot wind. It was sure to be of some bright color, usually red. Modern would-be cow-punchers do not willingly let this old kerchief die, and right often they overplay it. For the cowboy of the "movies," however, let us register an unqualified contempt. The real range would never have been safe for him.

A peculiar and distinctive feature of the cowboy's costume was his "chaps" *(chaparéjos)*. The chaps were two very wide and full-length trouser-legs made of heavy calfskin and connected by a narrow belt or strap. They were cut away entirely at front and back so that they

covered only the thigh and lower legs and did not heat the body as a complete leather garment would. They were intended solely as a protection against branches, thorns, briers, and the like, but they were prized in cold or wet weather. Sometimes there was seen, more often on the southern range, a cowboy wearing chaps made of skins tanned with the hair on; for the cowboy of the Southwest early learned that goatskin left with the hair on would turn the cactus thorns better than any other material. Later, the chaps became a sort of affectation on the part of new men on the range; but the old-time cowboy wore them for use, not as a uniform. In hot weather he laid them off.

In the times when some men needed guns and all men carried them, no pistol of less than 44-caliber was tolerated on the range, the solid framed 45-caliber being the one almost universally used. The barrel was eight inches long, and it shot a rifle cartridge of forty grains of powder and a blunt-ended bullet that made a terrible missile. This weapon descended from a belt worn loose resting upon the left hip and hanging low down on the right hip so that none of the weight came upon the abdomen. This was typical, for the cowboy was neither fancy gunman nor army officer. The latter carries the revolver on the left, the butt pointing forward.

An essential part of the cow-puncher's outfit was his "rope." This was carried in a close coil at the side of the saddle-horn, fastened by one of the many thongs scattered over the saddle. In the Spanish country it was called *reata* and even today is sometimes seen in the Southwest made of rawhide. In the South it was called a *lariat*. The modern rope is a well-made three-quarter-inch hemp rope about thirty feet in length, with a leather or raw-hide eye. The cowboy's quirt was a short heavy whip, the stock being of wood or iron covered with braided leather and carrying a lash made of two or three heavy loose thongs. The spur in the old days had a very large rowel with blunt teeth an inch long. It was often ornamented with little bells or oblongs of metal, the tinkling of which appealed to the childlike nature of the Plains rider. Their use was to lock the rowel.

His bridle—for, since the cowboy and his mount are inseparable, we may as well speak of his horse's dress also—was noticeable for its tremendously heavy and cruel curbed bit, known as the "Spanish bit." But in the ordinary riding and even in the exciting work of the old round-up and in "cutting out," the cowboy used the bit very little, nor exerted any pressure on the reins. He laid the reins against the neck of the pony opposite to the direction in which he wished it to go, merely turning his hand in the direction and inclining his body in the same way. He rode with the pressure of the knee and the inclination of the body and the light side-shifting of both reins. The saddle was the most important part of the outfit. It was a curious thing, this saddle developed by the cattle trade, and the world has no other like it. Its great weight—from thirty to forty pounds—was readily excusable when one remembers that it was not only seat but workbench for the cowman. A light saddle would be torn to pieces at the first rush of a maddened steer, but the sturdy frame of a cow-saddle would throw the heaviest bull on the range. The high cantle would give a firmness to the cowboy's seat when he snubbed a steer with a sternness sufficient to send it rolling heels over head. The high pommel, or "horn," steel-forged and covered with cross braids of leather, served as anchor post for this same steer, a turn of the rope about it accomplishing that purpose at once. The saddle-tree forked low down over the pony's back so that the saddle sat firmly and could not readily be pulled off. The great broad cinches bound the saddle fast till horse and saddle were practically one fabric. The strong wooden house of the old heavy stirrup protected the foot from being crushed by the impact of the herd. The form of the cow-saddle has changed but little, although today one sees a shorter seat and smaller horn, a "swell front" or roll, and a stirrup of open "ox-bow" pattern.

The round-up was the harvest of the range. The time of the calf round-up was in the spring after the grass had become good and after the calves had grown large enough for the branding. The State Cattle Association divided the entire State range into a number of round-up districts. Under an elected round-up captain were all the bosses in charge of the different ranch outfits sent by men having cattle in the round-up. Let us briefly draw a picture of this scene as it was.

Each cowboy would have eight or ten horses for his own use, for he had now before him the hardest riding of the year. When the cow-puncher went into the herd to cut out calves he mounted a fresh horse, and every few hours he again changed horses, for there was no horse which could long endure the fatigue of the rapid and intense work of cutting. Before the rider stretched a sea of interwoven horns, waving and whirling as the densely packed ranks of cattle closed in or swayed apart. It was no prospect for a weakling, but into it went the cow-puncher on his determined little horse, heeding not the plunging, crushing, and thrusting of the excited cattle. Down under the bulks of the herd, half hid in the whirl of dust, he would spy a little curly calf running, dodging, and twisting, always at the heels of its mother; and he would dart in after, following the two through the thick of surging and plunging beasts. The sharp-eyed pony would see almost as soon as his rider which cow was wanted and he needed small guidance from that time on. He would follow hard at her heels, edging her constantly toward the flank of the herd, at times nipping her hide as a reminder of his own superiority. In spite of herself the cow would gradually turn out toward the edge, and at last would be swept clear of the crush, the calf following close behind her. There was a whirl of the rope and the calf was laid by the heels and dragged to the fire where the branding irons were heated and ready.

Meanwhile other cow-punchers are rushing calves to the branding. The hubbub and turmoil increase. Taut ropes cross the ground in many directions. The cutting ponies pant and sweat, rear and plunge. The garb of the cowboy is now one of white alkali which hangs gray in his eyebrows and moustache. Steers bellow as they surge to and fro. Cows charge on their persecutors. Fleet yearlings break and run for the open, pursued by men who care not how or where they ride.

"The Herd Quitter" by Charles Marion Russell, 1897.

We have spoken in terms of the past. There is no calf round-up of the open range today. The last of the round-ups was held in Routt County, Colorado, several years ago, so far as the writer knows, and it had only to do with shifting cattle from the summer to the winter range.

After the calf round-up came the beef round-up, the cowman's final harvest. This began in July or August. Only the mature or fatted animals were cut out from the herd. This "beef cut" was held apart and driven on ahead from place to place as the round-up progressed. It was then driven in by easy stages to the shipping point on the railroad, whence the long trainloads of cattle went to the great markets.

In the heyday of the cowboy it was natural that his chief amusements should be those of the outdoor air and those more or less in line with his employment. He was accustomed to the sight of big game, and so had the edge of his appetite for its pursuit worn off. Yet he was a hunter, just as every Western man was a hunter in the times of the Western game. His weapons were the rifle, revolver, and rope; the latter two were always with him. With the rope at times he captured the coyote, and under special conditions he has taken deer and even antelope in this way, though this was of course most unusual and only possible under chance conditions of ground and cover. Elk have been roped by cowboys many times, and it is known that even the mountain sheep has been so taken, almost incredible as that may seem. The young buffalo were easy prey for the cowboy and these he often roped and made captive. In fact the beginnings of all the herds of buffalo now in captivity in this country were the calves roped and secured by cowboys; and these few scattered individuals of a grand race of animals remain as melancholy reminders alike of a national shiftlessness and an individual skill and daring.

The grizzly was at times seen by the cowboys on the range, and if it chanced that several cowboys were together it was not unusual to give him chase. They did not always rope him, for it was rarely that the nature of the country made this possible. Sometimes they roped him and wished they could let him go, for a grizzly bear is uncommonly active and straightforward in his habits at close quarters. The extreme difficulty of such a combat, however, gave it its chief fascination for the cowboy. Of course, no one horse could hold the bear after it was roped, but, as one after another came up, the bear was caught by neck and foot and body, until at last he was tangled and tripped and haled about till he was helpless, strangled, and nearly dead. It is said that cowboys have so brought into camp a grizzly bear, forcing him to half walk and half slide at the end of the ropes. No feat better than this could show the courage of the plainsman and of the horse which he so perfectly controlled.

Of such wild and dangerous exploits were the cowboy's amusements on the range. It may be imagined what were his amusements when he visited the "settlements." The cow-punchers, reared in the free life of the open air, under circumstances of the utmost freedom of individual action, perhaps came off the drive or round-up after weeks or months of unusual restraint or hardship, and felt that the time had arrived for them to "celebrate." Merely great rude children, as wild and untamed and untaught as the herds they led, they regarded their first look at the "settlements" of the railroads as a glimpse of a wider world. They pursued to the uttermost such avenues of new experience as lay before them, almost without exception avenues of vice. It is strange that the records of those days should be chosen by the public to be held as the measure of the American cowboy. Those days were brief, and they are long since gone. The American cowboy atoned for them by a quarter of a century of faithful labor.

The amusements of the cowboy were like the features of his daily surroundings and occupation—they were intense, large, Homeric. Yet, judged at his work, no higher type of employee ever existed, nor one more dependable. He was the soul of honor in all the ways of his calling. The very blue of the sky, bending evenly over all men alike, seemed to symbolize his instinct for justice. Faithfulness and manliness were his chief traits; his standard—to be a "square man."

Not all the open range will ever be farmed, but very much that was long thought to be irreclaimable has gone under irrigation or is being more or less successfully "dry-farmed." The man who brought water upon the arid lands of the West changed the entire complexion of a vast country and with it the industries of that country. Acres redeemed from the desert and added to the realm of the American farmer were taken from the realm of the American cowboy.

The West has changed. The curtain has dropped between us and its wild and stirring scenes. The old days are gone. The house dog sits on the hill where yesterday the coyote sang. There are fenced fields and in them stand sleek round beasts, deep in crops such as their ancestors never saw. In a little town nearby is the hurry and bustle of modern life. This town is far out upon what was called the frontier, long after the frontier has really gone. Guarding its ghost here stood a little army post, once one of the pillars, now one of the monuments of the West.

Out from the tiny settlement in the dusk of evening, always facing toward where the sun is sinking, might be seen riding, not so long ago, a figure we should know. He would thread the little lane among the fences, following the guidance of hands other than his own, a thing he would once have scorned to do. He would ride as lightly and as easily as ever, sitting erect and jaunty in the saddle, his reins held high and loose in the hand whose fingers turn up gracefully, his whole body free yet firm in the saddle with the seat of the perfect horseman. At the boom of the cannon, when the flag dropped fluttering down to sleep, he would rise in his stirrups and wave his hat to the flag. Then, toward the edge, out into the evening, he would ride on. The dust of his riding would mingle with the dusk of night. We could not see which was the one or the other. We could only hear the hoof-beats passing, boldly and steadily still, but growing fainter, fainter, and more faint.

CHAPTER SIX

THE KID

Walter Noble Burns

Billy the Kid, 1879 or 1880.

Billy the Kid's legend in New Mexico seems destined to a mellow and genial immortality like that which gilds the misdeeds and exaggerates the virtues of such ancient rogues as Robin Hood, Claude Duval, Dick Turpin, and Fra Diavolo. From the tales you hear of him everywhere, you might be tempted to fancy him the best-loved hero in the state's history. His crimes are forgotten or condoned, while his loyalty, his gay courage, his superman adventures are treasured in affectionate memory. Men speak of him with admiration; women extol his gallantry and lament his fate. A rude balladry in Spanish and English has grown up about him, and in every *placeta* in New Mexico, Mexican girls sing to their guitars songs of Billy the Kid. A halo has been clapped upon his scapegrace brow. The boy who never grew old has become a sort of symbol of frontier knight-errantry, a figure of eternal youth riding forever through a purple glamour of romance.

Gray-beard skald at boar's-head feast when the foaming goblets of mead went round the board in the gaunt hall of Vikings never sang to his wild harp saga more thrilling than the story of Billy the Kid. A boy is its hero: a boy when the tale begins, a boy when it ends; a boy born to battle and vendetta, to hatred and murder, to tragic victory and tragic defeat, and who took it all with a smile.

Fate set a stage. Out of nowhere into the drama stepped this unknown boy. Opposite him played Death. It was a drama of Death and the Boy. Death dogged his trail relentlessly. It was forever clutching at him with skeleton hands. It lay in ambush for him. It edged him to the gallows' stairs. By bullets, conflagration, stratagems, every lethal trick, it sought to compass his destruction. But the boy was not to be trapped. He escaped by apparent miracles; he was saved as if by necromancy. He laughed at Death. Death was a joke. He waved Death a jaunty good-bye and was off to new adventures. But again the inexorable circle closed. Now life seemed sweet. It beckoned to love and happiness. A golden vista opened before him. He set his foot upon the sunlit road. Perhaps for a moment the boy dreamed this drama was destined to a happy ending. But no. Fate prompted from the wings. The moment of climax was at hand. The boy had had his hour. It was Death's turn. And so the curtain.

Billy the Kid was the Southwest's most famous desperado and its last great outlaw. He died when he was twenty-one years old and was credited with having killed twenty-one men—a man for every year of his life. Few careers in pioneer annals have been more colorful; certain of his exploits rank among the classic adventures of the West. He lived at a transitional period of New Mexican history. His life closed the past; his death opened the present. His destructive and seemingly futile career served a constructive purpose: it drove home the lesson that New Mexico's prosperity could be built only upon a basis of stability and peace. After him came the great change for which he involuntarily had cleared the way. Law and order came in on the flash and smoke of the six-shooter that with one bullet put an end to the outlaw and to outlawry.

That a boy in a brief life-span of twenty-one years should have attained his sinister preeminence on a lawless and turbulent frontier would seem proof of a unique and extraordinary personality. He was born for his career. The mental and physical equipment that gave his genius for depopulation effectiveness and background and enabled him to survive in a tumultuous time of plots and murders was a birthright rather than an accomplishment. He had the desperado complex which, to endure for any appreciable time in his environment, combined necessarily a peculiarly intricate and enigmatic psychology with a dexterous trigger-finger.

Billy the Kid doubtless would fare badly under the microscope of psychoanalysis. Weighed in the delicate balance of psychiatry, he would be dropped, neatly labelled, into some category of split personality and abnormal psychosis. The desperado complex, of which he was an exemplar, may perhaps be defined as frozen egoism plus recklessness and minus mercy. In its less aggravated forms it is not uncommon. There are desperadoes of business, the pulpit, the drawing room. The business man who plots the ruin of his rival; the minister who consigns to eternal damnation all who disbelieve in his personal creed; the love pirate, who robs another woman of her husband; the speed-mad automobilist who disregards life and limb, are all desperado types. The lynching mob is a composite desperado. Among killers there are good and bad desperadoes; both equally deadly, one killing lawlessly and the other to uphold the law. Wild Bill won his reputation as an officer of the law, killing many men to establish peace. The good "bad man" had a definite place in the development of the West.

But in fairness to Billy the Kid he must be judged by the standards of his place and time. The part of New Mexico in which he passed his life was the most murderous spot in the West. The Lincoln County war, which was his background, was a culture-bed of many kinds and degrees of desperadoes. There were the embryo desperado whose record remained negligible because of lack of excuse or occasion for murder; the would-be desperado who loved melodrama and felt called upon, as an artist, to shed a few drops of blood to maintain the prestige of his melodrama; and the desperado of genuine spirit but mediocre craftsmanship whose climb toward the heights was halted abruptly by some other man an eighth of a second quicker on the trigger. All these men were as ruthless and desperate as Billy the Kid, but they lacked the afflatus that made him the finished master. They were journeymen mechanics laboriously carving notches on the handles of their guns. He was a genius painting his name in flaming colors with a six-shooter across the sky of the Southwest.

With his tragic record in mind, one might be pardoned for visualizing Billy the Kid as an inhuman monster reveling in blood. But this conception would do him injustice. He was a boy of bright, alert mind, generous, not unkindly, of quick sympathies. The steadfast loyalty of his friendships was proverbial. Among his friends he was scrupulously honest. Moroseness and sullenness were foreign to him. He was cheerful, hopeful, talkative, given to laughter. He was not addicted to swagger or braggadocio. He was quiet, unassuming, courteous. He was a great favorite with women, and in his attitude toward them he lived up to the best traditions of the frontier.

But hidden away somewhere among these pleasant human qualities was a hiatus in his character—a sub-zero vacuum—devoid of all human emotions. He was upon occasion the personification of merciless, remorseless deadliness. He placed no value on human life, least of all upon his own. He killed a man as nonchalantly as he smoked a cigarette. Murder did not appeal to Billy the Kid as tragedy; it was merely a physical process of pressing a trigger. If it seemed to him necessary to kill a man, he killed him and got the matter over with as neatly and with as little fuss as possible. In his murders, he observed no rules of etiquette and was bound by no punctilios of honor. As long as he killed a man he wanted to kill, it made no difference to him how he killed him. He fought fair and shot it out face to face if the occasion demanded but under other circumstances he did not scruple at assassination. He put a bullet through a man's heart as coolly as he perforated a tin can set upon a fence post. He had no remorse. No memories haunted him.

His courage was beyond question. It was a static courage that remained the same under all circumstances, a noon or at three o'clock in the morning. There are yellow spots in the stories of many of the West's most famous desperadoes. We are told that in certain desperate crises with the odds against them, they weakened and were no braver than they might have been when, for instance, the other man got the drop on them and they looked suddenly into the blackness of forty-four caliber death. But no tale has come down that Billy the Kid ever showed the "yellow streak." Every hour in his desperate life was the zero hour, and he was never afraid to die. "One chance in a million" was one of his favorite phrases, and more than once he took that chance with the debonair courage of a cavalier. Even those who hated him and the men who hunted him to his death admitted his absolute fearlessness.

But courage alone would not have stamped him as extraordinary in the Southwest where courage is a tradition. The quality that distinguished his courage from that of other brave men lay in a nerveless imperturbability. Nothing excited him. He had nerve but no nerves. He retained a cool, unruffled poise in the most thrilling crises. With death seemingly inevitable, his face remained calm; his steady hands gave no hint of quickened pulses; no unusual flash in his eyes—and eyes are accounted the Judas Iscariots of the soul—betrayed his emotions or his plans.

The secrets of Billy the Kid's greatness as a desperado—and by connoisseurs in such matters he was rated as an approach to the ideal desperado type—lay in a marvelous coordination between mind and body. He not only had the will but the skill to kill. Daring, coolness, and quick-thinking would not have served unless they had been combined with physical quickness and a marksmanship which enabled him to pink a man neatly between the eyes with a bullet at, say, thirty paces. He was not pitted against six-shooter amateurs but against experienced fighters adept themselves in the handling of weapons. The men he killed would have killed him if he had not been their master in a swifter deadliness. In times of danger, his mind was not only calm but singularly clear and nimble, watching like a hawk for an advantage and seizing it with incredible celerity. He was able to translate an impulse into action with the suave rapidity of a flash of light. While certain other men were a fair match for him in target practice, no man in the Southwest, it is said, could equal him in the lightning-like quickness with which he could draw a six-shooter from its holster and with the same movement fire with deadly accuracy. It may be remarked incidentally that shooting at a target is one thing and shooting at a man who happens to be blazing away at you is something entirely different; and Billy the Kid did both kinds of shooting equally well.

His appearance was not unprepossessing. He had youth, health, good nature, and a smile—a combination which usually results in a certain sort of good looks. His face was long and colorless except for the deep tan with which it had been tinted by sun, wind, and weather, and was of an asymmetry that was not unattractive. His hair was light brown, worn usually rather long and inclined to waviness. His eyes were gray, clear and steady. His upper front teeth were large and slightly prominent, and to an extent disfigured the expression of a well-formed mouth. His hands and feet were remarkably small. He was five feet eight inches tall, slender and well proportioned. He was unusually strong for his inches, having for a small man quite powerful arms and shoulders. He weighed, in condition, one hundred and forty pounds. When out on the range, he was as rough-looking as any other cowboy. In towns, among the quality-folk of the frontier, he dressed neatly and took not a little care in making himself personable. Many persons, especially women, thought him handsome. He was a great beau at fandangos and was considered a good dancer.

He had an air of easy, unstudied, devil-may-care insouciance which gave no hint of his dynamic energy. His movements were ordinarily deliberate and unhurried. But there was a certain element of calculation in everything he did. Like a billiardist who "plays position," he figured on what he might possibly have to do next. This foresightedness and forehandedness even in inconsequential matters provided him with a sort of subconscious mail armor. He was forearmed even when not forewarned; forever on guard.

Like all the noted killers of the West, Billy the Kid was of the blond type. Wild Bill Hickok, Ben Thompson, King Fisher, Henry Plummer, Clay Allison, Wyatt Earp, Doc Holliday, Frank and Jesse

James, the Youngers, the Daltons—the list of others is long—were all blond. There was not a pair of brown eyes among them. It was the gray and blue eye that flashed death in the days when the six-shooter ruled the frontier. This blondness of desperadoes is a curious fact, contrary to popular imagination and the traditions of art and the stage. The theatre immemorially has portrayed its unpleasant characters as black-haired and black-eyed. The popular mind associates swarthiness with villainy. Blue eyes and golden hair are, in the artistic cannon, a sort of heavenly hallmark. No artist has yet been so daring as to paint a winged cherub with raven tresses, and a search of the world's canvases would discover no brown-eyed angel. It may be remarked further, as a matter of incidental interest, that the West's bad men were never heavy, stolid, lowering brutes. Most of them were good-looking, some remarkably so. Wild Bill Hickok, beau ideal of desperadoes, was considered the handsomest man of his day on the frontier, and with his blue eyes and yellow hair falling on his shoulders, he moved through his life of trag-edies with something of the beauty of a Greek god. So much for fact versus fancy. Cold deadliness in Western history seems to have run to frosty colouring in eyes, hair, and complexion.

Though it is possible that the record of twenty-one killings attributed to Billy the Kid is exaggerated, there is strong reason to believe it true. He was remarkably precocious in homicide; he is said to have killed his first man when he was only twelve years old. He is sup-posed to have killed about twelve men before he appeared in Lincoln County. This early phase of his life is vague. From the outbreak of the Lincoln County war, his career is easily traceable and clearly authentic.

It is impossible now to name twenty-one men that he killed, though, if Indians be included, it is not difficult to cast up the ghastly total. It may be that in his record were secret murders of which only he himself knew. There are rife in New Mexico many unauthenticated stories in which the names of his victims are not given. One tale credits him with having killed five Mexicans in camp near Seven Rivers. Another has it that a number of the twenty or more unmarked graves on the banks of the Pecos at the site of John Chisum's old Bosque Grande ranch contain the dust of men the Kid sent to their long sleep.

The Kid himself claimed to have killed twenty-one. He made this statement unequivocably a number of times to a number of men and he was never regarded as a braggart or a liar.

"I have killed twenty-one men and I want to make it twenty-three before I die," he said a little before his death to Pete Maxwell at Fort

Portrait of Pat Garret

Sumner. "If I live long enough to kill Pat Garrett and Barney Mason, I'll be satisfied."

Sheriff Pat Garrett, who for several years was the Kid's close friend—and who killed him—placed the Kid's record at eleven. John W. Poe, who was with Garrett at the Kid's death, accepted the Kid's own statement. In a letter written to me shortly before his death in 1923, Poe said:

> Billy the Kid had killed more men than any man I ever knew or heard of during my fifty years in the Southwest. I cannot name the twenty-one men he killed; nor can any man alive to-day. I doubt if there ever was a man who could name them all except the Kid himself. He was the only man who knew exactly. He said he had killed twenty-one and I believe him.

Poe, who succeeded Pat Garrett as sheriff of Lincoln County and was at the time of his death president of the Citizens National Bank of Roswell, was a veteran man-hunter and knew the criminal element of the Southwest as few men did. If Poe, with his first-hand knowledge of the Kid, had faith in the Kid's own statement, it would seem fair grounds for presumption that the statement is true.

So the matter stands. With most of the actors in the old drama now dead and gone, it is safe to say the tragic conundrum of how many men fell before Billy the Kid's six-shooters will never be definitely answered. Certainly the list was long. And it is worth remembering that the Kid was only a boy when he died and, however his record is itemized, each item is a grave.

To realize the bizarre quality of Billy the Kid's character try to fancy yourself in his place. Suppose, if you please, that under stress of circumstances you had killed several men. Assume that you felt justified in these homicides. Very well. Would an easy conscience bring you peace of mind? No. If you did not regret the killings, you would regret profoundly the necessity for them. The thought of blood on your soul would forever haunt you. Your spirit would be shaken and shadowed by remorse.

But that would not be all. The relatives and friends of those you had killed would hate you. They would hound you everywhere with their hatred. They would dog your footsteps and lie in wait to take your life. They would watch with jungle eyes for an opportunity for revenge.

Nor would this fill the cup of your misery. You would have achieved the sinister reputation of a fighter and a killer. Men who had no cause of quarrel against you, to whom your killings had meant nothing, would look upon you as they might upon a dangerous beast, a menace to society, a being outside the pale of human sympathy and law. The pack would be ready at any time to fall upon you without mercy and tear you to pieces. You would approach every rock and tree with caution lest some hidden foe fire upon you. You would not dare sleep in the same bed twice. You would suspect every man of treachery. When you sat at meat, you would feel that Death sat across the table with hollow eyes fixed upon you. Any minute you might expect a bullet or the plunge of a knife driven by unutterable hatred. Fear would walk hand in hand with you and lie down with you at night. You could not smile; peace and happiness would be denied you; there would be no zest, no joy for you this side of the grave. In your despair, you would welcome death as an escape from the hopeless hell of your hunted, haunted life.

But Billy the Kid was not of the stuff of ordinary men. There must have been in him a remarkable capacity for forgetfulness; he might seem to have drunk every morning a nepenthe that drowned in oblivion all his yesterdays. For him there was no past. He lived in the present from minute to minute, yet he lived happily. He killed without emotion and he accepted the consequences of his killings without emotion. His murders were strong liquor that left no headache. Surrounded by enemies who would have killed him with joy, breathing an atmosphere of bitter hatred, in danger of violent death every moment, he went his way through life without remorse, unracked by nerves or memories, gay, light-hearted, fearless, always smiling.

If you would learn in what affectionate regard the people of New Mexico cherish the memory of Billy the Kid to-day, you have but to journey in leisurely fashion through the Billy the Kid country. Everyone will have a story to tell you of his courage, generosity, loyalty, light-heartedness, engaging boyishness. More than likely you yourself will fall under the spell of these kindly tales and, before you are aware, find yourself warming with romantic sympathy to the idealized picture of heroic and adventurous youth.

Sit, for instance, on one of the benches under the shade trees in the old square at Santa Fe where the wagon caravans used to end their long journey across the plains. Here the rich and poor of this ancient capital of the land of *mañana* and sunshine come every day to while away an hour and smoke and talk politics. Mention Billy the Kid to some leisurely burgher. Instantly his face will light up; he will cease his tirade against graft and corruption in high places and go off into interminable anecdotes. Yes, Billy the Kid lived here in Santa Fe when he was a boy. Many a time when he was an outlaw with a price on his head, he rode into town and danced all night at the dance hall over on Gallisteo Street. The house is still there; the pink adobe with the blue door and window shutters. Did the police attempt to arrest him? Not much. Those blue-coated fellows valued their hides. Why, that boy wasn't afraid of the devil. Say, once over at Anton Chico . . .

Or drop into some little adobe home in Puerta de Luna. Or in Santa Rosa. Or on the Hondo. Or anywhere between the Ratons and Seven Rivers. Perhaps the Mexican housewife will serve you with frijoles and tortillas and coffee with goat's milk. If you are wise in the ways of Mexicans, you will tear off a fragment of tortilla and, cupping it between your fingers, use it as a spoon to eat your frijoles that are red with chili pepper and swimming in soup rich with fat bacon grease.

But between mouthfuls of these beans of the gods—and you will be ready to swear they are that, else you are no connoisseur in beans—don't forget to make some casual reference to Billy the Kid. Then watch the face of your hostess. At mention of the magic name, she will smile softly and dream-light will come into her eyes.

"Billee the Keed? Ah, you have hear of heem? He was one gran' boy, señor. All Mexican pepul his friend. You nevair hear a Mexican say one word against Billee the Keed. Everybody love that boy. He was so kind-hearted, so generous, so brave. And so 'andsome. *Nombre de Dios!* Every leetle señorita was crazy about heem. They all try to catch that Billee the Keed for their sweetheart. Ah, many a pretty *muchacha* cry her eyes out when he is keel; and when she count her beads at Mass, she add a prayer for good measure for his soul to rest in peace. Poor Billee the Keed! He was good boy—*muy valiente, muy caballero."*

Or ask Frank Coe about him. You will find him a white-haired old man now on his fruit ranch in Ruidoso Cañon. He fought in the Lincoln County war by the Kid's side and as he tells his story you may sit in a rocking chair under the cottonwoods while the Ruidoso River sings its pleasant tune just back of the rambling, one-story adobe ranch house.

"Billy the Kid," says Coe, "lived with me for a while soon after he came to Lincoln County in the fall of 1877. Just a little before he went to work for Tunstall on the Feliz. No, he didn't work for me. Just lived with me. Riding the chuck line. Didn't have anywhere else special to stay just then. He did a lot of hunting that winter. Billy was a great hunter, and the hills hereabouts were full of wild turkey, deer, and cinnamon bear. Billy could hit a bear's eye so far away I could hardly see the bear.

"He was only eighteen years old, as nice-looking a young fellow as you'd care to meet, and certainly mighty pleasant company. Many a night he and I have sat up before a pine-knot fire swapping yarns. Yes, he had killed quite a few men even then, but it didn't seem to weigh on him. None at all. Ghosts, I reckon, never bothered Billy. He was about as cheerful a little hombre as I ever ran across. Not the grim, sullen kind; but full of talk, and it seemed to me he was laughing half his time.

"You never saw such shooting as that lad could do. Not a dead shot. I've heard about these dead shots but I never happened to meet one. Billy was the best shot with a six-shooter I ever saw, but he missed sometimes. Jesse Evans, who fought on the Murphy side, used to brag that he was as good a shot as the Kid, but I never thought so, and I knew Jesse and have seen him shoot. Jesse, by the way, used to say, too, that he wasn't afraid of Billy the Kid. Which was just another one of his brags. He was scared to death of the Kid, and once when they met in Lincoln, Billy made him take water and made him like it. Billy used to do a whole lot of practice shooting around the ranch, and had the barn peppered full of holes. I have heard people say they have seen him empty his shooter at a hat tossed about twenty feet into the air and hit it six times before it struck the ground. I won't say he couldn't do it, but I never saw him do it. One of his favorite stunts was to shoot at snowbirds sitting on fence posts along the road as he rode by with his horse at a gallop. Sometimes he would kill a half-a-dozen birds one after the other; and then he would miss a few. His average was about one in three. And I'd say that was mighty good shooting.

"Billy had had a little schooling, and he could read and write as well as anybody else around here. I never saw him reading any books, but he was a great hand to read newspapers whenever he could get hold of any. He absorbed a lot of education from his newspaper reading. He didn't talk like a backwoodsman. I don't suppose he knew much about the rules of grammar, but he didn't make the common, glaring mistakes of ignorant people. His speech was that of an intelligent and fairly well-educated man. He had a clean mind; his conversation was never coarse or vulgar; and while most of the men with whom he associated swore like pirates, he rarely used an oath.

"He was a free-hearted, generous boy. He'd give a friend the shirt off his back. His money came easy when it came; but sometimes it didn't come. He was a gambler and, like all gamblers, his life was chicken one day and feathers the next, a pocketful of money to-day and broke to-morrow. Monte was his favorite game; he banked the game or bucked it, depending on his finances. He was as slick a dealer as ever threw a card, and as a player, he was shrewd, usually lucky, and bet 'em high—the limit on every turn. While he stayed with me, he broke a Mexican monte bank every little while down the *cañon* at San Patricio. If he happened to lose, he'd take it like a good gambler and, like as not, crack a joke and walk away whistling with his hands rammed in his empty pockets. Losing his money never made him mad. To tell the truth, I never saw Billy the Kid mad in my life, and I knew him several years.

"Think what you please, the Kid had a lot of principle. He was about as honest a fellow as I ever knew outside of some loose notions about rustling cattle. This was stealing, of course, but I don't believe it struck him exactly that way. It didn't seem to have any personal element in it. There were the cattle running loose on the plains without any owner in sight or sign of ownership, except the brands, seeming

like part of the landscape. Billy, being in his fashion a sort of poten-
tate ruling a large portion of the landscape with his six-shooter, felt, I
suppose, like he had a sort of proprietary claim on those cattle, and it
didn't seem to him like robbery—not exactly—to run them off and
cash in on them at the nearest market. That's at least one way of fig-
uring it out. But as for other lowdown kinds of theft like sticking up
a lonely traveler on the highway, or burglarizing a house, or picking
pockets, he was just as much above that sort of thing as you or me. I'd
have trusted him with the last dollar I had in the world. One thing is
certain, he never stole a cent in his life from a friend."

The history of Billy the Kid already has been clouded by legend.
Less than fifty years after his death, it is not always easy to differentiate
fact from myth. Historians have been afraid of him, as if this boy of
six-shooter deadliness might fatally injure their reputations if they set
themselves seriously to write of a career of such dime-novel luridness.
As a consequence, history has neglected him. Fantastic details have
been added as the tales have been told and retold. He is already in
process of evolving into the hero of a Southwestern *Niebelungenlied*.
Such a mass of stories has grown about him that it seems safe to predict
that in spite of anything history can do to rescue the facts of his life,
he is destined eventually to be transformed by popular legend into the
Robin Hood of New Mexico—a heroic out-law endowed with every
noble quality fighting the battle of the common people against the
tyranny of wealth and power.

Innumerable stories in which Billy the Kid figures as a semi myth-
ical hero are to be picked up throughout New Mexico. They are told
at every camp fire on the range; they enliven the winter evenings in
every Mexican home. There is doubtless a grain of truth in every one,
but the troubadour touch is upon them all. You will not find them
in books, and their chief interest perhaps lies in the fact that they

are examples of oral legend kept alive in memory and passed on by the story-tellers of one generation to the story-tellers of the next in Homeric succession. They are folklore in the making. As each narrative adds a bit of drama here, a picturesque detail there, one wonders what form these legends will assume as time goes by, and in what heroic proportions Billy the Kid will appear in fireside fairy tales a hundred years or so from now.

CHAPTER SEVEN

HOPALONG NURSES A GROUCH

Clarence E. Mulford

"Hopalong Takes Command" by Frank Schoonover, 1905.

After the excitement incident to the affair at Powers' shack had died down and the Bar-20 outfit worked over its range in the old, placid way, there began to be heard low mutterings, and an air of peevish discontent began to be manifested in various childish ways. And it was all caused by the fact that Hopalong Cassidy had a grouch, and a big one. It was two months old and growing worse daily, and the signs threatened contagion. His foreman, tired and sick of the snarling, fidgety, petulant atmosphere that Hopalong had created on the ranch, and driven to desperation, eagerly sought some chance to get rid of the "sore-thumb" temporarily and give him an opportunity to shed his generous mantle of the blues. And at last it came.

No one knew the cause for Hoppy's unusual state of mind, although there were many conjectures, and they covered the field rather thoroughly; but they did not strike on the cause.

Even Red Connors, now well over all ill effects of the wounds acquired in the old ranch house, was forced to guess; and when Red had to do that about anything concerning Hopalong he was well warranted in believing the matter to be very serious.

Johnny Nelson made no secret of his opinion and derived from it a great amount of satisfaction, which he admitted with a grin to his foreman.

"Buck," he said, "Hoppy told me he went broke playing poker over in Grant with Dave Wilkes and them two Lawrence boys, an' that shore explains it all. He's got pack sores from carrying his unholy licking. It was due to come for him, an' Dave Wilkes is just the boy to deliver it. That's the whole trouble, an' I know it, an' I'm damned glad they trimmed him. But he ain't got no right of making us miserable because he lost a few measly dollars."

"Yo're wrong, son; dead, dead wrong," Buck replied. "He takes his beatings with a grin, an' money never did bother him. No poker game that ever was played could leave a welt on him like the one we all mourn, an' cuss. He's been doing something that he don't want us to know—made a fool of hisself some way, most likely, an' feels so ashamed that he's sore. I've knowed him too long an' well to believe that gambling had anything to do with it. But this little trip he's taking will fix him up all right, an' I couldn't 'a' picked a better man—or one that I'd rather get rid of just now."

"Well, lemme tell you it's blamed lucky for him that you picked him to go," rejoined Johnny, who thought more of the woeful absentee than he did of his own skin. "I was going to lick him, shore, if it went on much longer. Me an' Red an' Billy was going to beat him up good till he forgot his dead injuries an' took more interest in his friends."

Buck laughed heartily. "Well, the three of you might 'a' done it if you worked hard an' didn't get careless, but I have my doubts. Now look here—you've been hanging around the bunk house too blamed much lately. Henceforth an' hereafter you've got to earn your grub. Get out on that west line an' hustle."

"You know I've had a toothache!" snorted Johnny with a show of indignation, his face as sober as that of a judge.

"An' you'll have a stomach ache from lack of grub if you don't earn yore right to eat purty soon," retorted Buck. "You ain't had a toothache in yore whole life, an' you don't know what one is. G'wan, now, or I'll give you a backache that'll ache!"

"Huh! Devil of a way to treat a sick man!" Johnny retorted, but he departed exultantly, whistling with much noise and no music. But he was sorry for one thing: he sincerely regretted that he had not been present when Hopalong met his Waterloo. It would have been pleasing to look upon.

While the outfit blessed the proposed lease of range that took him out of their small circle for a time, Hopalong rode farther and farther into the northwest, frequently lost in abstraction which, judging by its effect upon him, must have been caused by something serious. He had not heard from Dave Wilkes about that individual's good horse which had been loaned to Ben Ferris, of Winchester. Did Dave think he had been killed or was still pursuing the man whose neck-kerchief had aroused such animosity in Hopalong's heart? Or had the horse actually been returned? The animal was a good one, a successful contender in all distances from one to five miles, and had earned its owner and backers much money—and Hopalong had parted with it as easily as he would have borrowed five dollars from Red. The story, as he had often reflected since, was as old as lying—a broken-legged horse, a wife dying forty miles away, and a horse all saddled which needed only to be mounted and ridden.

These thoughts kept him company for a day and when he dismounted before Stevenson's "Hotel" in Hoyt's Corners he summed up his feelings for the enlightenment of his horse.

"Damn it, bronc! I'd give ten dollars right now to know if I was a jackass or not," he growled.

"But he was an awful slick talker if he lied. An' I've got to go up an' face Dave Wilkes to find out about it!"

Mr. Cassidy was not known by sight to the citizens of Hoyt's Corners, however well versed they might be in his numerous exploits of wisdom and folly. Therefore the habitues of Stevenson's Hotel did not recognize him in the gloomy and morose individual who dropped his saddle on the floor with a crash and stamped over to the three-legged table at dusk and surlily demanded shelter for the night.

"Gimme a bed an' something to eat," he demanded, eyeing the three men seated with their chairs tilted against the wall. "Do I get 'em?" he asked, impatiently.

"You do," replied a one-eyed man, lazily arising and approaching him. "One dollar, now."

"An' take the rocks outen that bed—I want to sleep."

"A dollar per for every rock you find," grinned Stevenson, pleasantly. "There ain't no rocks in my beds," he added.

"Some folks likes to be rocked to sleep," facetiously remarked one of the pair by the wall, laughing contentedly at his own pun. He bore all the ear-marks of being regarded as the wit of the locality—every hamlet has one; I have seen some myself.

"Hee, hee, hee! Yo're a droll feller, Charley," chuckled Old John Ferris, rubbing his ear with unconcealed delight. "That's a good un."

"One drink, now," growled Hopalong, mimicking the proprietor, and glaring savagely at the "droll feller" and his companion. "An' mind that it's a good one," he admonished the host.

"It's better," smiled Stevenson, whereat Old John crossed his legs and chuckled again. Stevenson winked.

"Riding long?" he asked.

"Since I started."

"Going fur?"

"Till I stop."

"Where do you belong?" Stevenson's pique was urging him against the ethics of the range, which forbade personal questions.

Hopalong looked at him with a light in his eye that told the host he had gone too far. "Under my sombrero!" he snapped.

"Hee, hee, hee!" chortled Old John, rubbing his ear again and nudging Charley. "He ain't no fool, hey?"

"Why, I don't know, John; he won't tell," replied Charley.

Hopalong wheeled and glared at him, and Charley, smiling uneasily, made an appeal: "Ain't mad, are you?"

"Not yet," and Hopalong turned to the bar again, took up his liquor and tossed it off. Considering a moment he shoved the glass back again, while Old John tongued his lips in anticipation of a treat. "It is good—fill it again."

The third was even better and by the time the fourth and fifth had joined their predecessors Hopalong began to feel a little more cheerful. But even the liquor and an exceptionally well-cooked supper could not separate him from his persistent and set grouch. And of liquor he had already taken more than his limit. He had always boasted, with truth, that he had never been drunk, although there had been two occasions when he was not far from it. That was one doubtful luxury which he could not afford for the reason that there were men who would have been glad to see him, if only for a few seconds, when liquor had dulled his brain and slowed his speed of hand. He could never tell when and where he might meet one of these.

He dropped into a chair by a card table and, baffling all attempts to engage him in conversation, reviewed his troubles in a mumbled soliloquy, the liquor gradually making him careless. But of all the jumbled words his companions' diligent ears heard they recognized and retained only the bare term "Winchester"; and their conjectures were limited only by their imaginations.

Hopalong stirred and looked up, shaking off the hand which had aroused him. "Better go to bed, stranger," the proprietor was saying. "You an' me are the last two up. It's after twelve, an' you look tired and sleepy."

"Said his wife was sick," muttered the puncher. "Oh, what you saying?"

"You'll find a bed better'n this table, stranger—it's after twelve an' I want to close up an' get some sleep. I'm tired myself."

"Oh, that all? Shore I'll go to bed—like to see anybody stop me! Ain't no rocks in it, hey?"

"Nary a rock," laughingly reassured the host, picking up Hopalong's saddle and leading the way to a small room off the "office," his guest stumbling after him and growling about the rocks that lived in Winchester. When Stevenson had dropped the saddle by the window and departed, Hopalong sat on the edge of the bed to close his eyes for just a moment before tackling the labor of removing his clothes. A crash and a jar awakened him and he found himself on the floor with his back to the bed. He was hot and his head ached, and his back was skinned a little—and how hot and stuffy and choking the room had become! He thought he had blown out the light, but it still burned, and three-quarters of the chimney was thickly covered with soot. He was stifling and could not endure it any longer. After three attempts he put out the light, stumbled against his saddle and, opening the window, leaned out to breathe the pure air. As his lungs filled he chuckled wisely and, picking up the saddle, managed to get it and himself through the window and on the ground without serious mishap. He would ride for an hour, give the room time to freshen and cool off, and come back feeling much better. Not a star could be seen as he groped his way unsteadily towards the rear of the building, where he vaguely remembered having seen the corral as he rode up.

"Huh! Said he lived in Winchester an' his name was Bill—no, Ben Ferris," he muttered, stumbling towards a noise he knew was made by a horse rubbing against the corral fence. Then his feet got tangled up in the cinch of his saddle, which he had kicked before him, and after great labor he arose, muttering savagely, and continued on his wobbly way. "Goo' Lord, it's darker'n cats in—oof!" he grunted, recoiling from forcible contact with the fence he sought. Growling words unholy he felt his way along it and finally his arm slipped through an opening and he bumped his head solidly against the top bar of the gate. As he righted himself his hand struck the nose of a horse and closed mechanically over it. Cow-ponies look alike in the dark and he grinned jubilantly as he complimented himself upon finding his own so unerringly.

"Anything is easy, when you know how. Can't fool me, ol' cayuse," he beamed, fumbling at the bars with his free hand and getting them down with a fool's luck. "You can't do it—I got you firs', las', an' always; an' I got you good. Yessir, I got you good. Quit that rearing, you ol' fool! Stan' still, can't you?" The pony sidled as the saddle hit its back and evoked profane abuse from the indignant puncher as he risked his balance in picking it up to try again, this time successfully.

He began to fasten the girth, and then paused in wonder and thought deeply, for the pin in the buckle would slide to no hole but the first. "Huh! Getting fat, ain't you, piebald?" he demanded with withering sarcasm. "You blow yoreself up any more'n I'll bust you wide open!" heaving up with all his might on the free end of the strap, one knee pushing against the animal's side. The "fat" disappeared and Hopalong laughed. "Been learnin' new tricks, ain't you? Got smart since you been travellin', hey?" He fumbled with the bars again and got two of them back in place and then, throwing himself across the saddle as the horse started forward as hard as it could go, slipped off, but managed to save himself by hopping along the ground. As soon as he had secured the grip he wished he mounted with the ease of habit and felt for the reins. "G'wan now, an' easy—it's plumb dark an' my head's bustin'."

When he saddled his mount at the corral he was not aware that two of the three remaining horses had taken advantage of their opportunity and had walked out and made off in the darkness before he replaced the bars, and he was too drunk to care if he had known it.

The night air felt so good that it moved him to song, but it was not long before the words faltered more and more and soon ceased altogether and a subdued snore rasped from him. He awakened from time to time, but only for a moment, for he was tired and sleepy.

His mount very quickly learned that something was wrong and that it was being given its head. As long as it could go where it pleased it could do nothing better than head for home, and it quickened its pace towards Winchester. Some time after daylight it pricked up its ears and broke into a canter, which soon developed signs of irritation in its rider. Finally Hopalong opened his heavy eyes and looked around for his bearings. Not knowing where he was and too tired and miserable to give much thought to a matter of such slight importance, he glanced around for a place to finish his sleep. A tree some distance ahead of him looked inviting and towards it he rode. Habit made him picket the horse before he lay down and as he fell asleep he had vague recollections of handling a strange picket rope some time recently. The horse slowly turned and stared at the already snoring figure, glanced over the landscape, back to the queerest man it had ever met, and then fell to grazing in quiet content. A slinking coyote topped a rise a short distance away and stopped instantly, regarding the sleeping man with grave curiosity and strong suspicion. Deciding that there was nothing good to eat in that vicinity and that the man was carrying out a fell plot for the death of coyotes, it backed away out of sight and loped on to other hunting grounds.

* * *

Stevenson, having started the fire for breakfast, took a pail and departed towards the spring; but he got no farther than the corral gate, where he dropped the pail and stared. There was only one horse in the enclosure where the night before there had been four. He wasted no time in surmises, but wheeled and dashed back towards the hotel, and his vigorous shouts brought Old John to the door, sleepy and peevish. Old John's mouth dropped open as he beheld his habitually indolent host marking off long distances on the sand with each falling foot.

"What's got inter you?" demanded Old John.

"Our broncs are gone! Our broncs are gone!" yelled Stevenson, shoving Old John roughly to one side as he dashed through the doorway and on into the room he had assigned to the sullen and bibulous stranger. "I knowed it! I knowed it!" he wailed, popping out again as if on springs.

"He's gone, an' he's took our broncs with him, the measly, low-down dog! I knowed he wasn't no good! I could see it in his eye; an' he wasn't drunk, not by a darn sight. Go out an' see for yoreself if they ain't gone!" he snapped in reply to Old John's look. "Go on out, while I throw some cold grub on the table—won't have no time this morning to do no cooking. He's got five hours' start on us, an' it'll take some right smart riding to get him before dark; but we'll do it, an' hang him, too!"

"What's all this here rumpus?" demanded a sleepy voice from upstairs. "Who's hanged?" and Charley entered the room, very much interested. His interest increased remarkably when the calamity was made known and he lost no time in joining Old John in the corral to verify the news.

Old John waved his hands over the scene and carefully explained what he had read in the tracks, to his companion's great irritation, for Charley's keen eyes and good training had already told him all there was to learn; and his reading did not exactly agree with that of his companion.

"Charley, he's gone and took our cayuses; an' that's the very way he came—'round the corner of the hotel. He got all tangled up an' fell over there, an' here he bumped inter the palisade, an' dropped his saddle. When he opened the bars he took my roan gelding because it was the best an' fastest, an' then he let out the others to mix us up on the tracks. See how he went? Had to hop four times on one foot afore he could get inter the saddle. An' that proves he was sober, for no drunk could hop four times like that without falling down an' being drug to death. An' he left his own critter behind because he knowed it wasn't no good. It's all as plain as the nose on your face, Charley," and Old John proudly rubbed his ear. "Hee, hee, hee! You can't fool Old John, even if he is getting old. No, sir, b' gum."

Charley had just returned from inside the corral, where he had looked at the brand on the far side of the one horse left, and he waited impatiently for his companion to cease talking. He took quick advantage of the first pause Old John made and spoke crisply.

"I don't care what corner he came 'round, or what he bumped inter; an' any fool can see that. An' if he left that cayuse behind because he thought it wasn't no good, he was drunk. That's a Bar-20 cayuse, an' no hoss-thief ever worked for that ranch. He left it behind because he stole it; that's why. An' he didn't let them others out because he wanted to mix us up, neither. How'd he know if we couldn't tell the tracks of our own animals? He did that to make us lose time; that's what he did it for. An' he couldn't tell what bronc he took last night—it was too dark. He must 'a' struck a match an' seen where that Bar-20 cayuse was an' then took the first one nearest that wasn't it. An' now you tell me how the devil he knowed yourn was the fastest, which it ain't," he finished, sarcastically, gloating over a chance to rub it into the man he had always regarded as a windy old nuisance.

"Well, mebby what you said is—"

"Mebby nothing!" snapped Charley. "If he wanted to mix the tracks would he 'a' hopped like that so we couldn't help telling what cayuse he rode? He knowed we'd pick his trail quick, an' he knowed that every minute counted; that's why he hopped—why, yore roan was going like the wind afore he got in the saddle. If you don't believe it, look at them toe-prints!"

"H'm; reckon yo're right, Charley. My eyes ain't nigh as good as they once was. But I heard him say something 'bout Winchester," replied Old John, glad to change the subject. "Bet he's going over there, too. He won't get through that town on no critter wearing my brand. Everybody knows that roan, an'—"

"Quit guessing!" snapped Charley, beginning to lose some of the tattered remnant of his respect for old age. "He's a whole lot likely to head for a town on a stolen cayuse, now ain't he! But we don't care where he's heading; we'll foller the trail."

"Grub pile!" shouted Stevenson, and the two made haste to obey.

"Charley, gimme a chaw of yore tobacker," and Old John, biting off a generous chunk, quietly slipped it into his pocket, there to lay until after he had eaten his breakfast.

All talk was tabled while the three men gulped down a cold and uninviting meal. Ten minutes later they had finished and separated to find horses and spread the news; in fifteen more they had them and were riding along the plain trail at top speed, with three other men close at their heels. Three hundred yards from the corral they pounded out of an arroyo, and Charley, who was leading, stood up in his stirrups and looked keenly ahead. Another trail joined the one they were following and ran with and on top of it. This, he reasoned, had been made by one of the strays and would turn away soon. He kept his eyes looking well ahead and soon saw that he was right in his surmise, and without checking the speed of his horse in the slightest degree he went ahead on the trail of the smaller hoof-prints. In a moment Old John spurred forward and gained his side and began to argue hot-headedly.

"Hey! Charley!" he cried. "Why are you follering this track?" he demanded.

"Because it's his; that's why."

"Well, here, wait a minute!" and Old John was getting red from excitement. "How do you know it is? Mebby he took the other!"

"He started out on the cayuse that made these little tracks," retorted Charley, "an' I don't see no reason to think he swapped animules. Don't you know the prints of yore own cayuse?"

"Lawd, no!" answered Old John. "Why, I don't hardly ride the same cayuse the second day, straight hand-running. I tell you we ought to foller that other trail. He's just cute enough to play some trick on us."

"Well, you better do that for us," Charley replied, hoping against hope that the old man would chase off on the other and give his companions a rest.

"He ain't got sand enough to tackle a thing like that singlehanded," laughed Jed White, winking to the others.

Old John wheeled. "Ain't, hey! I am going to do that same thing an' prove that you are a pack of fools. I'm too old to be fooled by a common trick like that. An' I don't need no help—I'll ketch him all by myself, an' hang him, too!" And he wheeled to follow the other trail, angry and outraged. "Young fools," he muttered. "Why, I was fighting all round these parts afore any of 'em knowed the difference between day an' night!"

"Hard-headed old fool," remarked Charley, frowning, as he led the way again.

"He's gittin' old an' childish," excused Stevenson. "They say warn't nobody in these parts could hold a candle to him in his prime."

Hopalong muttered and stirred and opened his eyes to gaze blankly into those of one of the men who were tugging at his hands, and as he stared he started his stupefied brain sluggishly to work in an endeavor to explain the unusual experience. There were five men around him and the two who hauled at his hands stepped back and kicked him. A look of pained indignation slowly spread over his countenance as he realized beyond doubt that they were really kicking him, and with sturdy vigor. He considered a moment and then decided that such treatment was most unwarranted and outrageous and, further more, that he must defend himself and chastise the perpetrators.

"Hey!" he snorted, "what do you reckon yo're doing, anyhow? If you want to do any kicking, why kick each other, an' I'll help you! But I'll lick the whole bunch of you if you don't quit mauling me. Ain't you got no manners? Don't you know anything? Come 'round waking a feller up an' man-handling—"

"Get up!" snapped Stevenson, angrily.

"Why, ain't I seen you before? Somewhere? Sometime?" queried Hopalong, his brow wrinkling from intense concentration of thought. "I ain't dreaming; I've seen a one-eyed coyote som'ers, lately, ain't I?" he appealed, anxiously, to the others.

"Get up!" ordered Charley, shortly.

"An' I've seen you, too. Funny, all right."

"You've seen me, all right," retorted Stevenson. "Get up, damn you! Get up!"

"Why, I can't—my han's are tied!" exclaimed Hopalong in great wonder, pausing in his exertions to cogitate deeply upon this most remarkable phenomenon. "Tied up! Now what the devil do you think—"

"Use yore feet, you thief!" rejoined Stevenson roughly, stepping forward and delivering another kick. "Use yore feet!" he reiterated.

"Thief! Me a thief! Shore I'll use my feet, you yaller dog!" yelled the prostrate man, and his boot heel sank into the stomach of the offending Mr. Stevenson with sickening force and laudable precision. He drew it back slowly, as if debating shoving it farther. "Call me a thief, hey! Come poking 'round kicking honest punchers an' calling 'em names! Anybody want the other boot?" he inquired with grave solicitation.

Stevenson sat down forcibly and rocked to and fro, doubled up and gasping for breath, and Hopalong squinted at him and grinned with happiness. "Hear him sing! Reg'lar ol' brass band. Sounds like a cow pulling its hoofs outen the mud. Called me a thief, he did, just now. An' I won't let nobody kick me an' call me names. He's a liar, just a plain, squaw's dog liar, he—"

Two men grabbed him and raised him up, holding him tightly, and they were not over careful to handle him gently, which he naturally resented. Charley stepped in front of him to go to the aid of Stevenson and caught the other boot in his groin, dropping as if he had been shot. The man on the prisoner's left emitted a yell and loosed his hold to sympathize with a bruised shinbone, and his companion promptly knocked the bound and still intoxicated man down. Bill Thomas swore and eyed the prostrate figure with resentment and regret. "Hate to hit a man who can fight like that when he's loaded an' tied. I'm glad, all the same, that he ain't sober an' loose."

"An' you ain't going to hit him no more!" snapped Jed White, reddening with anger. "I'm ready to hang him, 'cause that's what he deserves, an' what we're here for, but I'm damned if I'll stand for any more mauling. I don't blame him for fighting, an' they didn't have no right to kick him in the beginning."

"Didn't kick him in the beginning," grinned Bill. "Kicked him in the ending. Anyhow," he continued seriously, "I didn't hit him hard—didn't have to. Just let him go an' shoved him quick."

"I'm just naturally going to clean house," muttered the prisoner, sitting up and glaring around.

"Untie my han's an' gimme a gun or a club or anything, an' watch yoreselves get licked. Called me a thief! What you fellers, then?—sticking me up an' busting me for a few measly dollars. Why didn't you take my money an' lemme sleep 'stead of waking me up an' kicking me? I wouldn't 'a' cared then."

"Come on, now; get up. We ain't through with you yet, not by a whole lot," growled Bill, helping him to his feet and steadying him. "I'm plumb glad you kicked 'em; it was coming to 'em."

"No, you ain't; you can't fool me," gravely assured Hopalong. "Yo're lying, an' you know it. What you going to do now? Ain't I got money enough? Wish I had an even break with you fellers! Wish my outfit was here!"

Stevenson, on his feet again, walked painfully up and shook his fist at the captive, from the side. "You'll find out what we want of you, you damned hoss-thief!" he cried. "We're going to tie you to that there limb so yore feet'll swing above the grass, that's what we're going to do."

Bill and Jed had their hands full for a moment and as they finally mastered the puncher, Charley came up with a rope. "Hurry up—no use dragging it out this way. I want to get back to the ranch some time before next week."

"Why I ain't no hoss-thief, you liar!" Hopalong yelled. "My name's Hopalong Cassidy of the Bar-20, an' when I tell my friends about what you've gone an' done they'll make you hard to find! You gimme any kind of a chance an' I'll do it all by myself, sick as I am, you yaller dogs!"

"Is that yore cayuse?" demanded Charley, pointing.

Hopalong squinted towards the animal indicated. "Which one?"

"There's only one there, you fool!"

"That so?" replied Hopalong, surprised. "Well, I never seen it afore. My cayuse is—is—where the devil is it?" he asked, looking around anxiously.

"How'd you get that one, then, if it ain't yours?"

"Never had it—'t ain't mine, nohow," replied Hopalong, with strong conviction. "Mine was a hoss."

"You stole that cayuse last night outen Stevenson's corral," continued Charley, merely as a matter of form. Charley believed that a man had the right to be heard before he died—it wouldn't change the result and so could not do any harm.

"Did I? Why—" his forehead became furrowed again, but the events of the night before were vague in his memory and he only stumbled in his soliloquy. "But I wouldn't swap my cayuse for that spavined, saddle-galled, ring-boned bone-yard! Why, it interferes, an' it's got the heaves something awful!" he finished triumphantly, as if an appeal to common sense would clinch things. But he made no headway against them, for the rope went around his neck almost before he had finished talking and a flurry of excitement ensued. When the dust settled he was on his back again and the rope was being tossed over the limb.

The crowd had been too busily occupied to notice anything away from the scene of their strife and were greatly surprised when they heard a hail and saw a stranger sliding to a stand not twenty feet from them. "What's this?" demanded the newcomer, angrily.

Charley's gun glinted as it swung up and the stranger swore again. "What you doing?" he shouted. "Take that gun off'n me or I'll blow you apart!"

"Mind yore business an' sit still!" Charley snapped. "You ain't in no position to blow anything apart. We've got a hoss-thief an' we're shore going to hang him regardless."

"An' if there's any trouble about it we can hang two as well as we can one," suggested Stevenson, placidly. "You sit tight an' mind yore own affairs, stranger," he warned.

Hopalong turned his head slowly. "He's a liar, stranger; just a plain, squaw's dog of a liar. An' I'll be much obliged if you'll lick hell outen 'em an' let—why hullo, hoss-thief!" he shouted, at once recognizing the other. It was the man he had met in the gospel tent, the man he had chased for a horse-thief and then swapped mounts with. "Stole any more cayuses?" he asked, grinning, believing that everything was all right now. "Did you take that cayuse back to Grant?" he finished.

"Han's up!" roared Stevenson, also covering the stranger. "So yo're another one of 'em, hey? We're in luck to-day. Watch him, boys, till I get his gun. If he moves, drop him quick."

"You damned fool!" cried Ferris, white with rage. "He ain't no thief, an' neither am I! My name's Ben Ferris an' I live in Winchester. Why, that man you've is Hopalong Cassidy—Cassidy, of the Bar-20!"

"Sit still—you can talk later, mebby," replied Stevenson, warily approaching him. "Watch him, boys!"

"Hold on!" shouted Ferris, murder in his eyes. "Don't you try that on me! I'll get one of you before I go; I'll shore get one! You can listen a minute, an' I can't get away."

"All right; talk quick."

Ferris pleaded as hard as he knew how and called attention to the condition of the prisoner. "If he did take the wrong cayuse he was too blind drunk to know it! Can't you see he was!" he cried.

"Yep; through yet?" asked Stevenson, quietly.

"No! I ain't started yet!" Ferris yelled. "He did me a good turn once, one that I can't never repay, an' I'm going to stop this murder or go with him. If I go I'll take one of you with me, an' my friends an' outfit'll get the rest."

"Wait till Old John gets here," suggested Jed to Charley. "He ought to know this feller."

"For the Lord's sake!" snorted Charley. "He won't show up for a week. Did you hear that, fellers?" he laughed, turning to the others.

"He knows me all right; an' he'd like to see me hung," replied the stranger. "I won't give up my guns, an' you won't lynch Hopalong Cassidy while I can pull a trigger. That's flat!" He began to talk feverishly to gain time and his eyes lighted suddenly. Seeing that Jed White was wavering, Stevenson ordered them to go on with the work they had come to perform, and he watched Ferris as a cat watches a mouse, knowing that he would be the first man hit if the stranger got a chance to shoot. But Ferris stood up very slowly in his stirrups so as not to alarm the five with any quick movement, and shouted at the top of his voice, grabbing off his sombrero and waving it frantically. A faint cheer reached his ears and made the lynchers turn quickly and look behind them. Nine men were tearing towards them at a dead gallop and had already begun to forsake their bunched-up formation in favor of an extended line. They were due to arrive in a very few minutes and caused Mr. Ferris' heart to overflow with joy.

CHAPTER EIGHT

DODGE

William MacLeod Raine

"Dodge City in 1878" by Robert Marr Wight.

It was in the days when the new railroad was pushing through the country of the plains Indians that a drunken cowboy got on the train at a way station in Kansas. John Bender, the conductor, asked him for his ticket. He had none, but he pulled out a handful of gold pieces.

"I wantta—g-go to—h-hell," he hiccoughed.

Bender did not hesitate an instant. "Get off at Dodge. One dollar, please."

Dodge City did not get its name because so many of its citizens were or had been, in the Texas phrase, on the dodge. It came quite respectably by way of its cognomen. The town was laid out by A. A. Robinson, chief engineer of the Atchison, Topeka & Santa Fe, and it was called for Colonel Richard I. Dodge, commander of the post at Fort Dodge and one of the founders of the place. It is worth noting this, because it is one of the few respectable facts in the early history of the cowboy capital. Dodge was a wild and uncurried prairie wolf, and it howled every night and all night long. It was gay and young and lawless. Its sense of humor was exaggerated and worked overtime. The crack of the six-shooter punctuated its hilarity ominously. Those who dwelt there were the valiant vanguard of civilization. For good or bad they were strong and forceful, many of them generous and big-hearted in spite of their lurid lives. The town was a hive of energy. One might justly use many adjectives about it, but the word respectable is not among them.

There were three reasons why Dodge won the reputation of being the wildest town the country had ever seen. In 1872 it was the end of the track, the last jumping-off spot into the wilderness, and in the days when transcontinental railroads were building across the desert the temporary terminus was always a gathering place of roughs and scalawags. The payroll was large, and gamblers, gunmen, and thugs gathered for the pickings. This was true of Hays, Abilene, Ogalala, and Kit Carson. It was true of Las Vegas and Albuquerque.

A second reason was that Dodge was the end of the long trail drive from Texas. Every year hundreds of thousands of longhorns were driven up from Texas by cowboys scarcely less wild than the hill steers they herded. The great plains country was being opened, and cattle were needed to stock a thousand ranches as well as to supply the government at Indian reservations. Scores of these trail herds were brought to Dodge for shipment, and after the long, dangerous, drive the punchers were keen to spend their money on such diversions as the town could offer. Out of sheer high spirits they liked to shoot up the town, to buck the tiger, to swagger from saloon to gambling hall, their persons garnished with revolvers, the spurs on their high-heeled boots jingling. In no spirit of malice they wanted it distinctly understood that they owned the town. As one of them once put it, he was born high up on the Guadaloupe, raised on prickly pear, had palled with alligators and quarreled with grizzlies.

Also, Dodge was the heart of the buffalo country. Here the hunters were outfitted for the chase. From here great quantities of hides were shipped back on the new railroad. R. M. Wright, one of the founders of the town and always one of its leading citizens, says that his firm alone shipped two hundred thousand hides in one season. He estimates the number of buffaloes in the country at more than twenty-five million, admitting that many as well informed as he put the figure at four times as many. Many times he and others travelled through the vast herds for days at a time without ever losing sight of them. The killing of buffaloes was easy, because the animals were so stupid. When one was shot they would mill round and round. Tom Nicholson killed 120 in forty minutes; in a little more than a month he slaughtered 2,173 of them. With good luck a man could earn a hundred dollars a day. If he had bad luck he lost his scalp.

The buffalo was to the Plains Indian food, fuel, and shelter. As long as there were plenty of buffaloes he was in Paradise. But he saw at once that this slaughter would soon exterminate the supply. He hated the hunter and battled against his encroachments. The buffalo hunter was an intrepid plainsman. He fought Kiowas, Comanches, and the Staked Plain Apaches, as well as the Sioux and the Arapahoe. Famous among these hunters were Kirk Jordan, Charles Rath, Emanuel Dubbs, Jack Bridges, and Curly Walker. Others even better known were the two Buffalo Bills (William Cody and William Mathewson) and Wild Bill.

These three factors then made Dodge: it was the end of the railroad, the terminus of the cattle trail from Texas, and the center of the buffalo trade. Together they made "the beautiful bibulous Babylon of the frontier," in the words of the editor of the *Kingsley Graphic*. There was to come a time later when the bibulous Babylon fell on evil days and its main source of income was old bones. They were buffalo-bones, gathered in wagons, and piled beside the track for shipment, hundreds and hundreds of carloads of them, to be used for fertilizer. (I have seen great quantities of such bones as far north as the Canadian Pacific line, corded for shipment to a factory.) It used to be said by way of derision that buffalo bones were legal tender in Dodge.

But that was in the far future. In its early years Dodge rode the wave of prosperity. Hays and Abilene and Ogalala had their day, but Dodge had its day and its night, too. For years it did a tremendous business. The streets were so blocked that one could hardly get through. Hundreds of wagons were parked in them, outfits belonging to freighters, hunters, cattlemen, and the government. Scores of camps surrounded the town in every direction. The yell of the cowboy and the weird oath of the bull-whacker and mule skinner were heard in the land. And for a time there was no law nearer than Hays City, itself a burg not given to undue quiet and peace.

Dodge was no sleepy village that could drowse along without peace officers. Bob Wright has set it down that in the first year of its history twenty-five men were killed and twice as many wounded. The elements that made up the town were too diverse for perfect harmony. The freighters did not like the railroad graders. The soldiers at the fort fancied themselves as scrappers. The cowboys and the buffalo hunters did not fraternize a little bit. The result was that Boot Hill began to fill up. Its inhabitants were buried with their boots on and without coffins.

There was another cemetery, for those who died in their beds. The climate was so healthy that it would have been very sparsely occupied those first years if it had not been for the skunks. During the early months Dodge was the city of camps. Every night the fires flamed up from the vicinity of hundreds of wagons. Skunks were numerous. They crawled at night into the warm blankets of the sleepers and bit the rightful owners when they protested. A dozen men died from these bites. It was thought at first that the animals were a special variety, known as the hydrophobia skunk. In later years I have sat around Arizona camp fires and heard this subject discussed heatedly. The Smithsonian Institute, appealed to as referee, decided that there was no such species and that deaths from the bites of skunks were probably due to blood poisoning caused by the foul teeth of the animal.

In any case, the skunks were only one half as venomous as the gunmen, judging by comparative staff statistics. Dodge decided it had to have law in the community. Jack Bridges was appointed first marshal.

Jack was a noted scout and buffalo hunter, the sort of man who would have peace if he had to fight for it. He did his sleeping in the afternoon, since this was a quiet time of the day. Someone shook him out of slumber one day to tell him that cowboys were riding up and down Front Street shooting the windows out of buildings. Jack sallied out, old buffalo gun in hand. The cowboys went whooping down the street across the bridge toward their camp. The old hunter took a long shot at one of them and dropped him. The cowboys buried the young fellow next day.

There was a good deal of excitement in the cow camps. If the boys could not have a little fun without some old donker, an old vinegaroon who couldn't take a joke, filling them full of lead it was a pretty howdy-do. But Dodge stood pat. The coroner's jury voted it justifiable homicide. In future the young Texans were more discreet. In the early days whatever law there was did not interfere with casualties due to personal differences of opinion provided the figure had no unusually sinister aspect.

The first wholesale killing was at Tom Sherman's dance hall. The affair was between soldiers and gamblers. It was started by a trooper named Hennessey, who had a reputation as a bad guy and a bully. He was killed, as were several others. The officers at the fort glossed over the matter, perhaps because they felt the soldiers had been to blame.

One of the lawless characters who drifted into Dodge the first year was Billy Brooks. He quickly established a reputation as a killer. My old friend Emanuel Dubbs, a buffalo hunter who "took the hides off'n" many a bison, is authority for the statement that Brooks killed or wounded fifteen men in less than a month after his arrival. Now Emanuel is a preacher (if he is still in the land of the living; I saw him last at Clarendon, Texas, ten years or so ago), but I cannot quite swallow that "fifteen." Still, he had a man for breakfast now and then and on one occasion four.

Brooks, by the way, was assistant marshal. It was the policy of the officials of these wild frontier towns to elect as marshal some conspicuous killer, on the theory that desperadoes would respect his prowess or if they did not would get the worst of the encounter.

Abilene, for instance, chose "Wild Bill" Hickok. Austin had its Ben Thompson. According to Bat Masterson, Thompson was the most dangerous man with a gun among all the bad men he knew—and Bat knew them all. Ben was an Englishman who struck Texas while still young. He fought as a Confederate under Kirby Smith during the Civil War and under Shelby for Maximilian. Later he was city marshal at Austin. Thompson was the man of the most cool effrontery. On one occasion, during a cattlemen's convention, a banquet was held at the leading hotel. The local congressman, a friend of Thompson, was not invited. Ben took exception to this and attended in person. By way of pleasantry he shot the plates in front of the diners. Later one of those present made humorous comment. "I always thought Ben was a game man. But what did he do? Did he hold up the whole convention of a thousand cattlemen? No, sir. He waited till he got forty or fifty of us poor fellows alone before he turned loose his wolf."

Of all the bad men and desperadoes produced by Texas, not one of them, not even John Wesley Hardin himself, was more feared than Ben Thompson. Sheriffs avoided serving warrants of arrest on him. It is recorded that once, when the county court was in session with a charge against him on the docket, Thompson rode into the room on a mustang. He bowed pleasantly to the judge and the court officials.

"Here I am, gents, and I'll lay all I'm worth that there's no charge against me. Am I right? Speak up, gents. I'm a little deaf."

There was a dead silence until at last the clerk of the court murmured, "No charge."

A story is told that on one occasion Ben Thompson met his match in the person of the young English remittance man playing cards with him. The remittance man thought he caught Thompson cheating and discreetly said so. Instantly Thompson's .44 covered him. For some unknown reason the gambler gave the lad a chance to retract.

"Take it back—and quick," he said grimly.

Every game in the house was suspended while all eyes turned on the daredevil boy and the hard-faced desperado. The remittance man went white, half rose from his seat, and shoved his head across the table toward the revolver.

"Shoot and be damned. I say you cheat," he cried hoarsely.

Thompson hesitated, laughed, shoved the revolver back into its holster, and ordered the youngster out of the house.

Perhaps the most amazing escape on record is that when Thompson, fired at by Mark Wilson at a distance of ten feet from a double-barreled shotgun loaded with buckshot, whirled instantly, killed him, and an instant later shot through the forehead Wilson's friend Mathews, though the latter had ducked behind the bar to get away. The second shot was guesswork plus quick thinking and accurate aim. Ben was killed a little later, in company with his friend King Fisher, another bad man, at the Palace Theatre. A score of shots were poured into them by a dozen men waiting in ambush. Both men had become so dangerous that their enemies could not afford to let them live.

King Fisher was the humorous gentleman who put up a signboard at the fork of a public road bearing the legend:

THIS IS KING FISHER'S ROAD. TAKE THE OTHER.

It is said that those traveling that way followed his advice. The other road might be a mile or two farther, but they were in no hurry. Another amusing little episode in King Fisher's career is told. He had had some slight difficulty with a certain bald-headed man. Fisher shot him and carelessly gave the reason that he wanted to see whether a bullet would glance from a shiny pate.

El Paso in its wild days chose Dallas Stoudenmire for marshal, and after he had been killed, John Selman. Both of them were noted killers. During Selman's régime John Wesley Hardin came to town. Hardin had twenty-seven notches on his gun and was the worst man killer Texas had ever produced. He was at the bar of a saloon shaking dice when Selman shot him from behind. One year later Deputy United States Marshal George Scarborough killed Selman in a duel. Shortly after this Scarborough was slain in a gunfight by "Kid" Curry, an Arizona bandit.

What was true of these towns was true, too, of Albuquerque and Las Vegas and Tombstone. Each of them chose for peace officers men who were "sudden death" with a gun. Dodge did exactly the same thing. Even a partial list of its successive marshals reads like a fighting roster. In addition to Bridges and Brooks may be named Ed and Bat Masterson, Wyatt Earp, Billy Tilghman, Ben Daniels, Mysterious Dave Mathers, T. C. Nixon, Luke Short, Charlie Bassett, W. H. Harris, and Sughrue brothers, all of them famous as fighters in a day when courage and proficiency with weapons were a matter of course. On one occasion the superintendent of the Santa Fe suggested to the city dads of Dodge that it might be a good thing to employ marshals less notorious. Dodge begged leave to differ. It felt that the best way to "settle the hash" of desperadoes was to pit against them fighting machines more efficient, bad men more deadly than themselves.

The word "bad" does not necessarily imply evil. One who held the epithet was known as one dangerous to oppose. He was unafraid, deadly with a gun, and hard as nails. He might be evil, callous, treacherous, revengeful as an Apache. Dave Mathers fitted this description. He might be a good man, kindly, gentle, never taking more than his fighting chance. This was Billy Tillman to a T.

We are keeping Billy Brooks waiting. But let that go. Let us look first at "Mysterious Dave." Bob Wright has set it down that Mathers had more dead men to his credit than any other man in the West. He slew seven by actual count in one night, in one house, according to Wright. Mathers had a very bad reputation. But his courage could blaze up magnificently. While he was deputy marshal word came that the Henry gang of desperadoes were terrorizing a dance hall. Into that hall walked Dave, beside his chief Tom Carson. Five minutes later out reeled Carson, both arms broken, his body shot through and through, a man with only five minutes to live. When the smoke in the hall cleared away Mathers might have been seen beside two handcuffed prisoners, one of them wounded. In a circle around him were four dead cowpunchers of the Henry outfit.

"Uncle" Billy Tilghman died the other day at Cromwell, Oklahoma, a victim of his own fearlessness. He was shot to death while taking a revolver from a drunken prohibition agent. If he had been like many other bad men he would have shot the fellow down at the first sign of danger. But that was never Tilghman's way. It was his habit to make arrests without drawing a gun. He cleaned up Dodge during the three years while he was marshal. He broke up the Doolin gang, killing Bill Raidler and "Little" Dick in personal duels and capturing Bill Doolin, the leader. Bat Masterson said that during Tilghman's term as sheriff of Lincoln County, Oklahoma, he killed, captured, or drove from the country more criminals than any other official that section had ever had. Yet "Uncle" Billy never used a gun except reluctantly. Time and again he gave the criminal the first shot, hoping the man would surrender rather than fight. Of all the old frontier sheriffs none holds a higher place than Billy Tilghman.

After which diversion we return to Billy Brooks, a "gent" of an impatient temperament, not used to waiting, and notably quick on the trigger. Mr. Dubbs records that late one evening in the winter '72–'73 he returned to Dodge with two loads of buffalo meat. He finished his business, ate supper, and started to smoke a postprandial pipe. The sound of a fusillade in an adjoining dance hall interested him since he had been deprived of the pleasures of metropolitan life for some time and had had to depend upon Indians for excitement. (Incidentally, it may be mentioned that they furnished him with a reasonable amount. Not long after this three of his men were caught, spread-eagled, and tortured by Indians. Dubbs escaped after a hair raising ride and arrived at Adobe Walls in time to take part in the historic defense of that post by a handful of buffalo hunters against many hundred tribesmen.) From the building burst four men. They started across the railroad track to another dance hall, one frequented by Brooks. Dubbs heard the men mention the name of Brooks, coupling it with an oath. Another buffalo hunter named Fred Singer joined Dubbs. They followed the strangers, and just before the four reached the dance hall Singer shouted a warning to the marshal. This annoyed the unknown four, and they promptly exchanged shots with the buffalo hunters. What then took place was startling in the sudden drama of it.

Billy Brooks stood in bold relief in the doorway, a revolver in each hand. He fired so fast that Dubbs says the sounds were like a company discharging weapons. When the smoke cleared Brooks still stood in the same place. Two of the strangers were dead and two mortally wounded. They were brothers. They had come from Hays City to avenge the death of a fifth brother shot down by Brooks some time before.

Mr. Brooks had a fondness for the fair sex. He and Browney, the yardmaster, took a fancy to the same girl. Captain Drew, she was called, and she preferred Browney. Whereupon Brooks naturally shot him in the head. Perversely, to the surprise of everybody, Browney recovered and was soon back at his old job.

Brooks seems to have held no grudge at him from making light of his marksmanship in this manner. At any rate, his next affair was with Kirk Jordan, the buffalo hunter. This was a very different business. Jordan had been in a hundred tight holes. He had fought Indians time and again. Professional killers had no terror for him. He threw down his big buffalo gun on Brooks, and the latter took cover. Barrels of water had been placed along the principal streets for fire protection. These had saved several lives during shooting scrapes. Brooks ducked behind one, and the ball from Jordan's gun plunged into it. The marshal dodged into a store, out of the rear door, and into a livery stable.

He was hidden under a bed. Alas! for a large reputation gone glimmer-
ing. Mr. Brooks fled to the fort, took the train from the siding, and
shook forever the dust of Dodge from his feet. Whither he departed a
deponent sayeth not.

How do I explain this? I don't. I record a fact. Many gunmen were
at one time or another subject to these panics during which the yellow
streak showed. Not all of them by any means, but a very consider-
able percentage. They swaggered boldly, killed recklessly. Then one day
some quiet little man with a cold gray eye called the turn on them, after
which they oozed out of the surrounding scenery.

Owen P. White gives it on the authority of Charlie Siringo that
Bat Masterson sang small when Clay Allison of the Panhandle, he of
the well-notched gun, drifted into Dodge and inquired for the city
marshal. But the old-timers at Dodge do not bear this out. Bat was at
the Adobe Walls fight, one of fourteen men who stood off five hundred bucks of the Cheyenne, Comanche, and Kiowa tribes. He scouted
for miles. He was elected sheriff of Ford County, with headquarters at
Dodge when only twenty-two years of age. It was a tough assignment,
and Bat executed it to the satisfaction of all concerned except the element he cowed.

Personally, I never met Bat until his killing days were past. He was
dealing faro at a gambling house in Denver when I, a young reporter,
first had the pleasure of looking into his cold blue eyes. It was a notable
fact that all the frontier bad men had eyes either gray or blue, often a
faded blue, expressionless, hard as jade.

It is only fair to Bat that the old-timers of Dodge do not accept the
Siringo point of view about him. Wright said of him that he was absolutely fearless and no trouble hunter. "Bat is a gentleman by instinct, of
pleasant manners, good address, and mild until aroused, and then, for
God's sake, look out. He is a leader of men, has much natural ability,

and good hard common sense. There is nothing low about him. He is high-toned and broad-minded, cool and brave." I give this opinion for what it is worth.

In any case, he was a most efficient sheriff. Dave Rudabaugh, later associated with Billy the Kid in New Mexico, staged a train robbery at Kingsley, Kansas, a territory not in Bat's jurisdiction. However, Bat set out in pursuit with a posse. A near-blizzard was sweeping the country. Bat made for Lovell's cattle camp, on the chance that the bandits would be forced to take shelter there. It was a good guess. Rudabaugh's outfit rode in, stiff and half frozen, and Bat captured the robbers without firing a shot. This was one of many captures Bat made.

He had a deep sense of loyalty to his friends. On two separate occasions he returned to Dodge, after having left the town, to straighten out difficulties for his friends or to avenge them. The first time was when Luke Short, who ran a gambling house in Dodge, had a difficulty with Mayor Webster and his official family. Luke appears to have held the opinion that the cards were stacked against him and that this was a trouble out of which he could not shoot himself. He wired Bat Masterson and Wyatt Earp to come to Dodge. They did, accompanied by another friend or two. The mayor made peace on terms dictated by Short.

Bat's second return to Dodge was caused by a wire from his brother James, who ran a dance hall in partnership with a man named Peacock. Masterson wanted to discharge the bartender, Al Updegraph, a brother-in-law of the other partner. A serious difficulty loomed in the offing. Wherefore James called for help. Bat arrived at eleven one sunny morning, another gunman at heel. At three o'clock he entrained for Tombstone, Arizona, James beside him. The interval had been busy one. On the way up from the station (always known then as the depot), the two men met Peacock and Updegraph.

No amenities were exchanged. It was strictly business. Bullets began to sing at once. The men stood across the street from each other and emptied their weapons. Oddly enough, Updegraph was the only one wounded. This little matter attended to, Bat surrendered himself, was fined three dollars for carrying concealed weapons, and released. He ate dinner, disposed of his brother's interest in the saloon, and returned to the station.

Bat Masterson was a friend of Theodore Roosevelt, who was given to admiring men with "guts," such men as Pat Garrett, Ben Daniels, and Billy Tilghman. Mr. Roosevelt offered Masterson a place as United States Marshal of Arizona. The ex-sheriff declined it. "If I took it," he explained, "I'd have to kill some fool boy who wanted to get a reputation by killing me." The President then offered Bat a place as Deputy United States Marshal of New York, and this was accepted. From that time Masterson became a citizen of the Empire State. For seventeen years he worked on a newspaper there and died a few years since with a pen in his hand. He was respected by the entire newspaper fraternity.

Owing to the pleasant habit of the cowboys of shooting up the town they were required, when entering the city limits, to hand over their weapons to the marshal. The guns were deposited at Wright & Beverly's Store, in a rack built for the purpose, and receipts given for them. Sometimes a hundred six-shooters would be there at once. These were never returned to their owners unless the cowboys were sober.

To be a marshal of one of these fighting frontier towns was no post to be sought for by a supple politician. The place called for a chilled iron nerve and an uncanny skill with the Colt. Tom Smith, one of the gamest men and best officers who ever wore a star on the frontier, was killed in the performance of his duty. Colonel Breackenridge says that Smith, marshal of Abilene before "Wild Bill," was the gamest man he ever knew. He was a powerful, athletic man who would arrest, himself unarmed, the most desperate characters. He once told Breackenridge that anyone could bring in a dead man but it took a good officer to take lawbreakers while they were alive. In this he differed from Hickok who did not take chances. He brought his men in dead. Nixon, assistant marshal at Dodge, was murdered by "Mysterious Dave" Mathers, who himself once held the same post. Ed Masterson, after displaying conspicuous courage many times, was mortally wounded April 9, 1878, by two desperate men, Jack Wagner and Alf Walker, who were terrorizing Front Street. Bat reached the scene a few minutes later and heard the story. As soon as his brother had died Bat went after the desperadoes, met them, and killed them both.

The death of Ed Masterson shocked the town. Civil organizations passed resolutions of respect. During the funeral, which was the largest ever held in Dodge, all business houses were closed. It is not on record that anybody regretted the demise of the marshal's assassins.

Among those who came to Dodge each season to meet the Texas cattle drive were Ben and Bill Thompson, gamblers who ran a faro bank. Previously they had been accustomed to go to Ellsworth, while that point was the terminus of the drive. Here they had ruled with a high hand, killed the sheriff, and made their getaway safely. Bill got into a shooting affray at Ogalala. He was badly wounded and was carried to the hotel. It was announced openly that he would never leave town alive. Ben did not dare go to Ogalala, for his record there outlawed him. He came to Bat Masterson.

Bat knew Bill's nurse and arranged a plan for campaign. A sham battle was staged at the big dance hall, during the excitement of which Bat and the nurse carried the wounded man to the train, got him to a sleeper, and into a bed. Buffalo Bill met them the next day at North Platte. He had relays of teams stationed on the road, and he and Bat guarded the sick man during the long ride bringing him safely to Dodge.

A portrait of Bat Masterson by Robert Marr Wright, 1913.

Emanuel Dubbs ran a roadhouse not far from Dodge about this time. He was practising with his six-shooter one day when a splendidly built young six-footer rode up to his place. The stranger watched him as he fired at the tin cans he had put on fence posts. Presently the young fellow suggested he throw a couple of the cans up in the air. Dubbs did so. Out flashed the stranger's revolvers. There was a roar of exploding shots. Dubbs picked up the cans. Four shots had been fired. Two bullets had drilled through each can.

"Better not carry a six-shooter till you learn to shoot," Bill Cody suggested, as he put his guns back into their holsters. "You'll be a living temptation to some bad man." Buffalo Bill was on his way back to the North Platte.

Life at Dodge was not all tragic. The six-shooter roared in the land a good deal, but there were very many citizens who went quietly about their business and took no part in the nightlife of the town. It was entirely optional with the individual. The little city had its legitimate theatres as well as its hurdy-gurdy houses and gambling dens. There was the Lady Gay, for instance, a popular vaudeville resort. There were well-attended churches. But Dodge boiled so with exuberant young life, often inflamed by bad liquor, that both theatre and church were likely to be the scenes of unexpected explosions.

A drunken cowboy became annoyed at Eddie Foy. While the comedian was reciting "Kalamazoo in Michigan" the puncher began bombarding the frail walls from the outside with a .45 Colt's revolver. Eddie made a swift strategic retreat. A deputy marshal was standing near the cow-puncher, who was astride a plunging horse. The deputy fired twice. The first shot missed. The second brought the rider down. He was dead before he hit the ground. The deputy apologized later for his marksmanship, but he added by way of explanation, "the bronc sure was sunfishin' plenty."

The killing of Miss Dora Hand, a young actress of much promise, was regretted by everybody in Dodge. A young fellow named Kennedy, the son of a rich cattleman, shot her unintentionally while he was trying to murder James Kelly. He fled. A posse composed of Sheriff Masterson, William Tilghman, Wyatt Earp, and Charles Bassett took the trail. They captured the man after wounding him desperately. He was brought back to Dodge, recovered, and escaped. His pistol arm was useless, but he used the other well enough to slay several other victims before someone made an end of him.

The gay good spirits of Dodge found continual expression in practical jokes. The wilder these were the better pleased was the town. "Mysterious Dave" was the central figure in one. An evangelist was conducting a series of meetings. He made a powerful magnetic appeal, and many were the hard characters who walked the sawdust trail. The preacher set his heart on converting Dave Mathers, the worst of bad men and a notorious scoffer. The meetings prospered. The church grew too small for the crowds and adjourned to a dance hall. Dave became interested. He went to hear Brother Johnson preach. He went a second time and a third. "He certainly preaches like the Watsons and goes for sin all spraddled out," Dave conceded. Brother Johnson grew hopeful. It seemed possible that this brand could be snatched from the burning. He preached directly at Dave, and Dave buried his head in his hands and sobbed. The preacher said he was willing to die if he could convert this one vile sinner. Others of the deacons agreed that they too, would not object to going straight to heaven with the knowledge that Dave had been saved.

"They were right excited an' didn't know straight up," an old-timer explained. "Dave, he looked so whipped his ears flopped. Finally he rose, an' said, 'I've got yore company, friends. Now, while we're all saved I reckon we better start straight for heaven. First off, the preacher; then the deacons; me last.' Then Dave whips out a whoppin' big gun and starts to shootin'. The preacher went right through a window an' took it with him. He was sure in some hurry. The deacons hunted cover. Seemed like they was willin' to postpone taking that through ticket to heaven. After that they never did worry anymore about Dave's soul."

Many rustlers gathered around Dodge in those days. The most notorious of these was a gang of more than thirty under the leadership of Dutch Henry and Tom Owens, two of the most desperate outlaws ever known in Kansas. A posse was organized to run down this gang under the leadership of Dubbs, who had lost some of his stock. Before starting, the posse telephoned Hays City to organize a company to head off the rustlers. Twenty miles west of Hays the posse overtook the rustlers. A bloody battle ensued, during which Owens and several other outlaws were killed and Dutch Henry wounded six times. Several of the posse were also shot. The story has a curious sequel. Many years later, when Emanuel Dubbs was county judge of Wheeler County, Texas, Dutch Henry came to his house and stayed there several days. He was a thoroughly reformed man. Not many years ago Dutch Henry died in Colorado. He was a man with many good qualities. Even in his outlaw days he had many friends among the law-abiding citizens.

After the battle with Henry Owens gang rustlers operated much more quietly, but they did not cease stealing. One night three men were hanged on a cottonwood on Saw Log Creek, ten or twelve miles from Dodge. One of these was a young man of a good family who had drifted into rustling and had been carried away by the excitement of it. Another of the three was the son of Tom Owens. To this day the place is known as Horse Thief Cañon. During its years of prosperity many eminent men visited Dodge, including Generals Sherman and Sheridan, President Hayes and General Miles. Its reputation had extended far and wide. It was the wild and woolly cowboy capital of the Southwest, a place to quicken the blood of any man. Nearly all that gay, hard-riding company of cowpunchers, buffalo hunters, bad men, and pioneers have vanished into yesterday's seven thousand years. But certainly Dodge once had its day and its night of glory. No more rip-roaring town ever bucked the tiger.

PART THREE

CLASSIC AUTHORS

CHAPTER NINE

THE QUEST BEGINS

Max Brand

"You know the old place on the other side of the range?"

"Like a book. I got pet names for all the trees."

"There's a man there I want."

"Logan?"

"No. His name is Bard."

"H-m! Any relation to the old bird that was partners with you back about the year one?"

"I want Anthony Bard brought here," said Drew, entirely overlooking the question.

"Easy. I can make the trip in a buckboard and I'll dump him in the back of it."

"No. He's got to *ride* here, understand?"

"A dead man," said Nash calmly, "ain't much good on a hoss."

"Listen to me," said Drew, his voice lowering to a sort of musical thunder, "if you harm a hair of this lad's head I'll—I'll break you in two with my own hands."

And he made a significant gesture as if he were snapping a twig between his fingers. Nash moistened his lips, then his square, powerful jaw jutted out.

"Which the general idea is me doing baby talk and sort of hypnotizing this Bard feller into coming along?"

"More than that. He's got to be brought here alive, untouched, and placed in that chair tied so that he can't move hand or foot for ten minutes while I talk."

"Nice, quiet day you got planned for me, Mr. Drew."

The grey man considered thoughtfully.

"Now and then you've told me of a girl at Eldara—I think her name is Sally Fortune?"

"Right. She begins where the rest of the calico leaves off."

"H-m! that sounds familiar, somehow. Well, Steve, you've said that if you had a good start you think the girl would marry you."

"I think she *might*."

"She pretty fond of you?"

"She knows that if I can't have her I'm fast enough to keep everyone else away."

"I see. A process of elimination with you as the eliminator. Rather an odd courtship, Steve?"

The cowpuncher grew deadly serious.

"You see, I love her. There ain't no way of bucking out of that. So do nine out of ten of all the boys that've seen her. Which one will she pick? That's the question we all keep askin', because of all the contrary, freckle-faced devils with the heart of a man an' the smile of a woman, Sally has 'em all beat from the drop of the barrier. One feller has money; another has looks; another has a funny line of talk. But I've got the fastest gun. So Sally sees she's due for a complete outfit of black mournin' if she marries another man while I'm alive; an' that keeps her thinkin'. But if I had the price of a start in the world—why, maybe she'd take a long look at me."

"Would she call one thousand dollars in cash a start in the world—and your job as foreman of my place, with twice the salary you have now?"

Steve Nash wiped his forehead.

He said huskily: "A joke along this line don't bring no laugh from me, governor."

"I mean it, Steve. Get Anthony Bard tied hand and foot into this house so that I can talk to him safely for ten minutes, and you'll have everything I promise. Perhaps more. But that depends."

The blunt-fingered hand of Nash stole across the table.

"If it's a go, shake, Mr. Drew."

A mighty hand fell in his, and under the pressure he set his teeth. Afterward he covertly moved his fingers and sighed with relief to see that no permanent harm had been done.

"Me speakin' personal, Mr. Drew, I'd of give a lot to seen you when you was ridin' the range. This Bard—he'll be here before sunset to-morrow."

"Don't jump to conclusions, Steve. I've an idea that before you count your thousand you'll think that you've been underpaid. That's straight."

"This Bard is something of a man?"

"I can say that without stopping to think."

"Texas?"

"No. He's a tenderfoot, but he can ride a horse as if he was sewed to the skin, and I've an idea that he can do other things up to the same standard. If you can find two or three men who have silent tongues and strong hands, you'd better take them along. I'll pay their wages, and big ones. You can name your price."

But Nash was frowning.

"Now and then I talk to the cards a bit, Mr. Drew, and you'll hear fellers say some pretty rough things about me, but I've never asked for no odds against any man. I'm not going to start now."

"You're a hard man, Steve, but so am I; and hard men are the kind I take to. I know that you're the best foreman who ever rode this range and I know that when you start things you generally finish them. All that I ask is that you bring Bard to me in this house. The way you do it is your own problem. Drunk or drugged, I don't care how, but get him here unharmed. Understand?"

"Mr. Drew, you can start figurin' what you want to say to him now. I'll get him here—safe! And then Sally—"

"If money will buy her you'll have me behind you when you bid."

"When shall I start?"

"Now."

"So-long, then."

He rose and passed hastily from the room, leaning forward from the hips like a man who is making a start in a foot-race.

Straight up the stairs he went to his room, for the foreman lived in the big house of the rancher. There he took a quantity of equipment from a closet and flung it on the bed. Over three selections he lingered long.

The first was the cartridge belt, and he tried over several with con-scientious care until he found the one which received the cartridges with the greatest ease. He could flip them out in the night, automati-cally as a pianist fingers the scale in the dark.

Next he examined lariats painfully, inch by inch, as though he were going out to rope the stanchest steer that ever roamed the range. Already he knew that those ropes were sound and true throughout, but he took no chances now. One of the ropes he discarded because one or two strands in it were, or might be, a trifle frayed. The other he took alternately and whirled with a broad loop, standing in the center of the room. Of the set one was a little more supple, a little more durable, it seemed. This he selected and coiled swiftly.

Last of all he lingered—and longest—over his revolvers. Six in all, he set them in a row along the bed and without delay threw out two to begin with. Then he fingered the others, tried their weight and balance, slipped cartridges into the cylinders and extracted them again, whirled the cylinders, and examined the minutest parts of the actions.

They were all such guns as an expert would have turned over with shining eyes, but finally he threw one aside into the discard; the cylin-der revolved just a little too hard. Another was abandoned after much handling of the remaining three because to the delicate touch of Nash it seemed that the weight of the barrel was a gram more than in the other two; but after this selection it seemed that there was no possible choice between the final two.

So he stood in the center of the room and went through a series of odd gymnastics. Each gun in turn he placed in the holster and then jerked it out, spinning it on the trigger guard around his second finger, while his left hand shot diagonally across his body and "fanned" the hammer. Still he could not make his choice, but he would not aban-don the effort. It was an old maxim with him that there is in all the world one gun which is the best of all and with which even a novice can become a "killer."

He tried walking away, whirling as he made his draw, and levelling the gun on the door-knob. Then without moving his hand, he lowered his head and squinted down the sights. In each case the bead was drawn to a center shot. Last of all he weighed each gun; one seemed a trifle lighter—the merest shade lighter than the other. This he slipped into the holster and carried the rest of his apparatus back to the closet from which he had taken it.

Still the preparation had not ended. Filling his cartridge belt, every cartridge was subject to a rigid inspection. A full half hour was wasted in this manner. Wasted, because he rejected not one of the many he examined. Yet he seemed happier after having made his selection, and went down the stairs, humming softly.

Out to the barn he went, lantern in hand. This time he made no comparison of horses but went directly to an ugly-headed roan, long of leg, vicious of eye, thin-shouldered, and with hips that slanted sharply down. No one with a knowledge of fine horse-flesh could have looked on this brute without aversion. It did not have even size in its favor. A wild, free spirit, perhaps, might be the reason; but the animal stood with hanging head and pendant lower lip. One eye was closed and the other only half opened. A blind affection, then, made him go to this horse first of all.

No, his greeting was to jerk his knee sharply into the ribs of the roan, which answered with a grunt and swung its head around with bared teeth, like an angry dog. "Damn your eyes!" roared the hoarse voice of Steve Nash, "stand still or I'll knock you for a goal!"

The ears of the mustang flattened close to its neck and a devil of hate came up in its eyes, but it stood quiet, while Nash went about at a judicious distance and examined all the vital points. The hooves were sound, the backbone prominent, but not a high ridge from famine or much hard riding, and the indomitable hate in the eyes of the mustang seemed to please the cowpuncher.

It was a struggle to bridle the beast, which was accomplished only by grinding the points of his knuckles into a tender part of the jowl to make the locked teeth open.

In saddling, the knee came into play again, rapping the ribs of the brute repeatedly before the wind, which swelled out the chest to false proportions, was expelled in a sudden grunt, and the cinch whipped up taut. After that Nash dodged the flying heels, chose his time, and vaulted into the saddle.

The mustang trotted quietly out of the barn. Perhaps he had had his fill of bucking on that treacherous, slippery wooden floor, but once outside he turned loose the full assortment of the cattle-pony's tricks. It was only ten minutes, but while it lasted the cursing of Nash was loud and steady, mixed with the crack of his murderous quirt against the roan's flanks. The bucking ended as quickly as it had begun, and they started at a long canter over the trail.

* * *

Mile after mile of the rough trail fell behind him, and still the pony shambled along at a loose trot or a swinging canter; the steep upgrades it took at a steady jog and where the slopes pitched sharply down, it wound among the rocks with a faultless sureness of foot.

Certainly the choice of Nash was well made. An Eastern horse of blood over a level course could have covered the same distance in half the time, but it would have broken down after ten miles of that hard trail.

Dawn came while they wound over the crest of the range, and with the sun in their faces they took the downgrade. It was well into the morning before Nash reached Logan. He forced from his eye the contempt which all cattlemen feel for sheepherders.

"I s'pose you're here askin' after Bard?" began Logan without the slightest prelude.

"Bard? Who's he?"

Logan considered the other with a sardonic smile.

"Maybe you been ridin' all night jest for fun?"

"If you start usin' your tongue on me, Logan, you'll wear out the snapper on it. I'm on my way to the A Circle Y."

"Listen; I'm all for old man Drew. You know that. Tell me what Bard has on him?"

"Never heard the name before. Did he rustle a couple of your sheep?"

Logan went on patiently: "I knew something was wrong when Drew was here yesterday but I didn't think it was as bad as this."

"What did Drew do yesterday?"

"Came up as usual to potter around the old house, I guess, but when he heard about Bard bein' here he changed his mind sudden and went home."

"That's damn queer. What sort of a lookin' feller is this Bard?"

"I don't suppose you know, eh?" queried Logan ironically. "I don't suppose the old man described him before you started, maybe?"

"Logan, you poor old hornless maverick, d'you think I'm on some-body's trail? Don't you know I've been through with that sort of game for a hell of a while?"

"When rocks turn into ham and eggs I'll trust you, Steve. I'll tell you what I done to Bard, anyway. Yesterday, after he found that Drew had been here and gone he seemed sort of upset; tried to keep it from me, but I'm too much used to judgin' changes of weather to be fooled by any tenderfoot that ever used school English. Then he hinted around about learnin' the way to Eldara, because he knows that town is pretty close to Drew's place, I guess. I told him; sure I did. He should of gone due west, but I sent him south. There *is* a south trail, only it takes about three days to get to Eldara."

"Maybe you think that interests me. It don't."

Logan overlooked this rejoinder, saying: "Is it his scalp you're after?"

"Your ideas are like nest-eggs, Logan, an' you set over 'em like a hen. They look like eggs; they feel like eggs; but they don't never hatch. That's the way with your ideas. They look all right; they sound all right; but they don't mean nothin'. So-long."

But Logan merely chuckled wisely. He had been long on the range.

As Nash turned his pony and trotted off in the direction of the A Circle Y ranch, the sheepherder called after him: "What you say cuts both ways, Steve. This feller Bard looks like a tenderfoot; he sounds like a tenderfoot; but he ain't a tenderfoot."

Feeling that this parting shot gave him the honors of the meeting, he turned away whistling with such spirit that one of his dogs, over-hearing, stood still and gazed at his master with his head cocked wisely to one side.

His eastern course Nash pursued for a mile or more, and then swung sharp to the south. He was weary, like his horse, and he made no attempt to start a sudden burst of speed. He let the pony go on at the same tireless jog, clinging like a bulldog to the trail.

About midday he sighted a small house cuddled into a hollow of the hills and made toward it. As he dismounted, a tow-headed, spin-dling boy lounged out of the doorway and stood with his hands shoved carelessly into his little overall pockets.

"Hello, young feller."

"'Lo, stranger."

"What's the chance of bunking here for three or four hours and gettin' a good feed for the hoss?"

"Never better. Gimme the hoss; I'll put him up in the shed. Feed him grain?"

"No, you won't put him up. I'll tend to that."

"Looks like a bad 'un."

"That's it."

"But a sure goer, eh?"

"Yep."

He led the pony to the shed, unsaddled him, and gave him a small feed. The horse first rolled on the dirt floor and then started methodically on his fodder. Having made sure that his mount was not "off his feed," Nash rolled a cigarette and strolled back to the house with the boy.

"Where's the folks?" he asked.

"Ma's sick, a little, and didn't get up to-day. Pa's down to the corral, cussing mad. But I can cook you up some chow."

"All right son. I got a dollar here that'll buy you a pretty good store knife."

The boy flushed so red that by contrast his straw colored hair seemed positively white.

"Maybe you want to pay me?" he suggested fiercely. "Maybe you think we're squatters that run a hotel?"

Recognizing the true Western breed even in this small edition, Nash grinned.

"Speakin' man to man, son, I didn't think that, but I thought I'd sort of feel my way."

"Which I'll say you're lucky you didn't try to feel your way with pa; not the way he's feelin' now."

In the shack of the house he placed the best chair for Nash and set about frying ham and making coffee. This with crackers, formed the meal. He watched Nash eat for a moment of solemn silence and then the foreman looked up to catch a meditative chuckle from the youngster.

"Let me in on the joke, son."

"Nothin'. I was just thinkin' of pa."

"What's he sore about? Come out short at poker lately?"

"No; he lost a hoss. Ha, ha, ha!"

He explained: "He's lost his only standin' joke, and now the laugh's on pa!"

Nash sipped his coffee and waited. On the mountain desert one does not draw out a narrator with questions.

"There was a feller come along early this mornin' on a lame hoss," the story began. "He was a sure enough tenderfoot—leastways he looked it an' he talked it, but he wasn't."

The familiarity of this description made Steve sit up a trifle straighter.

"Was he a ringer?"

"Maybe. I dunno. Pa meets him at the door and asks him in. What d' you think this feller comes back with?"

The boy paused to remember and then with twinkling eyes he mimicked: "'That's very good of you, sir, but I'll only stop to make a trade with you—this horse and some cash to boot for a durable mount out of your corral. The brute has gone lame, you see.'

"Pa waited and scratched his head while these here words sort of sunk in. Then says very smooth: 'I'll let you take the best hoss I've got, an' I won't ask much cash to boot.'

"I begin wonderin' what pa was drivin' at, but I didn't say nothin'— jest held myself together and waited.

"'Look over there to the corral,' says pa, and pointed. 'They's a hoss that ought to take you wherever you want to go. It's the best hoss I've ever had.'

"It *was* the best horse pa ever had, too. It was a piebald pinto called Jo, after my cousin Josiah, who's jest a plain bad un and raises hell when there's any excuse. The piebald, he didn't even need an excuse. You see, he's one of them hosses that likes company. When he leaves the corral he likes to have another hoss for a runnin' mate and he was jest as tame as anything. I could ride him; anybody could ride him. But if you took him outside the bars of the corral without company, first thing he done was to see if one of the other hosses was comin' out to join him. When he seen that he was all laid out to make a trip by himself he jest nacherally started in to raise hell. Which Jo can raise more hell for his size than any hoss I ever seen.

"He's what you call an eddicated bucker. He don't fool around with no pauses. He jest starts in and figgers out a situation and then he gets busy slidin' the gent that's on him off'n the saddle. An' he always used to win out. In fact, he was known for it all around these parts. He begun nice and easy, but he worked up like a fiddler playin' a favorite piece, and the end was the rider lyin' on the ground.

"Whenever the boys around here wanted any excitement they used to come over and try their hands with Jo. We used to keep a pile of arnica and stuff like that around to rub them up with and tame down the bruises after Jo laid 'em cold on the ground. There wasn't never anybody could ride that hoss when he was started out alone.

"Well, this tenderfoot, he looks over the hoss in the corral and says: 'That's a pretty fine mount, it seems to me. What do you want to boot?'

"'Aw, twenty-five dollars in enough,' says pa.

"'All right,' says the tenderfoot, 'here's the money.'

"And he counts it out in pa's hand.

"He says: 'What a little beauty! It would be a treat to see him work on a polo field.'

"Pa says: 'It'd be a treat to see this hoss work anywhere.'

"Then he steps on my foot to make me wipe the grin off'n my face.

"Down goes the tenderfoot and takes his saddle and flops it on the piebald pinto, and the piebald was jest as nice as milk. Then he leads him out'n the corral and gets on.

"First the pinto takes a look over his shoulder like he was waiting for one of his pals among the hosses to come along, but he didn't see none. Then the circus started. An' b'lieve me, it was some circus. Jo hadn't had much action for some time, an' he must have used the wait thinkin' up new ways of raisin' hell.

"There ain't enough words in the Bible to describe what he done. Which maybe you sort of gather that he *had* to keep on performin', because the tenderfoot was still in the saddle. He was. An' he never pulled leather. No, sir, he never touched the buckin' strap, but jest sat there with his teeth set and his lips twistin' back—the same smile he had when he got into the saddle. But pretty soon I s'pose Jo had a chance to figure out that it didn't do him no particular harm to be alone.

"The minute he seen that he stopped fightin' and started off at a gallop the way the tenderfoot wanted him to go, which was over there.

"'Damn my eyes!' says pa, an' couldn't do nuthin' but just stand there repeatin' that with variations because with Jo gone there wouldn't be no drawin' card to get the boys around the house no more. But you're lookin' sort of sleepy, stranger?"

"I am," answered Nash.

"Well, if you'd seen that show you wouldn't be thinkin' of sleep. Not for some time."

"Maybe not, but the point is I didn't see it. D'you mind if I turn in on that bunk over there?"

"Help yourself," said the boy. "What time d'you want me to wake you up?"

"Never mind; I wake up automatic. S'long, Bud."

He stretched out on the blankets and was instantly asleep.

* * *

At the end of three hours he awoke as sharply as though an alarm were clamoring at his ear. There was no elaborate preparation for renewed activities. A single yawn and stretch and he was again on his feet. Since the boy was not in sight he cooked himself an enormous meal, devoured it, and went out to the mustang.

The roan greeted him with a volley from both heels that narrowly missed the head of Nash, but the cowpuncher merely smiled tolerantly.

"Feelin' fit agin, eh, damn your soul?" he said genially, and picking up a bit of board, fallen from the side of the shed, he smote the mustang mightily along the ribs. The mustang, as if it recognized the touch of the master, pricked up one ear and side-stepped. The brief rest had filled it with all the old, vicious energy.

For once more, as soon as they rode clear of the door, there ensued a furious struggle between man and beast. The man won, as always, and the roan, dropping both ears flat against its neck, trotted sullenly out across the hills.

In that monotony of landscape, one mile exactly like the other, no landmarks to guide him, no trail to follow, however faintly worn, it was strange to see the cowpuncher strike out through the vast distances of the mountain-desert with as much confidence as if he were travelling on a paved street in a city. He had not even a compass to direct him but he seemed to know his way as surely as the birds know the untracked paths of the air in the seasons of migration.

Straight on through the afternoon and during the long evening he kept his course at the same unvarying dog-trot until the flush of the sunset faded to a stern grey and the purple hills in the distance turned blue with shadows. Then, catching the glimmer of a light on a hillside, he turned toward it to put up for the night.

In answer to his call a big man with a lantern came to the door and raised his light until it shone on a red, bald head and a portly figure. His welcome was neither hearty nor cold; hospitality is expected in the mountain-desert. So Nash put up his horse in the shed and came back to the house.

The meal was half over, but two girls immediately set a plate heaped with fried potatoes and bacon and flanked by a mighty cup of jet-black coffee on one side and a pile of yellow biscuits on the other. He nodded to them, grunted by way of expressing thanks, and sat down to eat.

Beside the tall father and the rosy-faced mother, the family consisted of the two girls, one of them with her hair twisted severely close to her head, wearing a man's blue cotton shirt with the sleeves rolled up to a pair of brown elbows. Evidently she was the boy of the family and to her fell the duty of performing the innumerable chores of the ranch, for her hands were thick with work and the tips of the fingers blunted. Also she had that calm, self-satisfied eye which belongs to the workingman who knows that he has earned his meal.

Her sister monopolized all the beauty and the grace, not that she was either very pretty or extremely graceful, but she was instinct with the challenge of femininity like a rare scent. It lingered about her, it enveloped her ways; it gave a light to her eyes and made her smile exquisite. Her clothes were not of much finer material than her sister's, but they were cut to fit, and a bow of crimson ribbon at her throat was as effective in that environment as the most costly orchids on an evening gown.

She was armed in pride this night, talking only to her mother, and then in monosyllables alone. At first it occurred to Steve that his coming had made her self-conscious, but he soon discovered that her pride was directed at the third man at the table. She at least maintained a pretense of eating, but he made not even a sham, sitting miserably, his mouth hard set, his eyes shadowed by a tremendous frown. At length he shoved back his chair with such violence that the table trembled.

"Well," he rumbled, "I guess this lets me out. S'long."

And he strode heavily from the room; a moment later his cursing came back to them as he rode into the night.

"Takes it kind of hard, don't he?" said the father.

And the mother murmured: "Poor Ralph!"

"So you went an' done it?" said the mannish girl to her sister.

"What of it?" snapped the other.

"He's too good for you, that's what of it."

"Girls!" exclaimed the mother anxiously. "Remember we got a guest!"

"Oh," said she of the strong brown arms, "I guess we can't tell him nothin'; I guess he had eyes to be seein' what's happened."

She turned calmly to Steve.

"Lizzie turned down Ralph Boardman—poor feller!"

"Sue!" cried the other girl.

"Well, after you done it, are you ashamed to have it talked about? You make me sore, I'll tell a man!"

"That's enough, Sue," growled the father.

"What's enough?"

"We ain't goin' to have no more show about this. I've had my supper spoiled by it already."

"I say it's a rotten shame," broke out Sue, and she repeated, "Ralph's too good for her. All because of a city dude—a tenderfoot!"

In the extremity of her scorn her voice drawled in a harsh murmur.

"Then take him yourself, if you can get him!" cried Lizzie. "I'm sure I don't want him!"

Their eyes blazed at each other across the table, and Lizzie, having scored an unexpected point, struck again.

"I think you've always had a sort of hankerin' after Ralph—oh, I've seen your eyes rollin' at him."

The other girl colored hotly through her tan.

"If I was fond of him I wouldn't be ashamed to let him know, you can tell the world that. And I wouldn't keep him trottin' about like a little pet dog till I got tired of him and give him up for the sake of a greenhorn who"—her voice lowered to a spiteful hiss—"kissed you the first time he even seen you!"

In vain Lizzie fought for her control; her lip trembled and her voice shook.

"I hate you, Sue!"

"Sue, ain't you ashamed of yourself?" pleaded the mother.

"No, I ain't! Think of it; here's Ralph been sweet on Liz for two years an' now she gives him the go-by for a skinny, affected dude like that feller that was here. And *he's* forgot you already, Liz, the minute he stopped laughing at you for bein' so easy."

"Ma, are you goin' to let Sue talk like this—right before a stranger?"

"Sue, you shut up!" commanded the father.

"I don't see nobody that can make me," she said, surly as a grown boy. "I can't make any more of a fool out of Liz than that tenderfoot made her!"

"Did he," asked Steve, "ride a piebald mustang?"

"D'you know him?" breathed Lizzie, forgetting the tears of shame which had been gathering in her eyes.

"Nope. Jest heard a little about him along the road."

"What's his name?"

Then she coloured, even before Sue could say spitefully: "Didn't he even have to tell you his name before he kissed you?"

"He did! His name is—Tony!"

"Tony!"—in deep disgust. "Well, he's dark enough to be a dago! Maybe he's a foreign count, or something, Liz, and he'll take you back to live in some castle or other."

But the girl queried, in spite of this badinage: "Do you know his name?"

"His name," said Nash, thinking that it could do no harm to betray as much as this, "is Anthony Bard, I think."

"And you don't know him?"

"All I know is that the feller who used to own that piebald mustang is pretty mad and cusses every time he thinks of him."

"He didn't steal the hoss?"

This with more bated breath than if the question had been: "He didn't kill a man?" for indeed horse-stealing was the greater crime.

Even Nash would not make such an accusation directly, and therefore he fell back on an innuendo almost as deadly.

"I dunno," he said non-committedly, and shrugged his shoulders.

With all his soul he was concentrating on the picture of the man who conquered a fighting horse and flirted successfully with a pretty girl the same day; each time riding on swiftly from his conquest. The clues on this trail were surely thick enough, but they were of such a nature that the pleasant mind of Steve grew more and more thoughtful.

* * *

In fact, so thoughtful had Nash become, that he slept with extraordinary lightness that night and was up at the first hint of day. Sue appeared on the scene just in time to witness the last act of the usual drama of bucking on the part of the roan, before it settled down to the mechanical dog-trot with which it would wear out the ceaseless miles of the mountain-desert all day and far into the night, if need be.

Nash now swung more to the right, cutting across the hills, for he presumed that by this time the tenderfoot must have gotten his bearings and would head straight for Eldara. It was a stiff two-day journey, now, the whole first day's riding having been a worse than useless detour; so the bulldog jaw set harder and harder, and the keen eyes squinted as if to look into the dim future.

Once each day, about noon, when the heat made even the desert and the men of the desert drowsy, he allowed his imagination to roam freely, counting the thousand dollars over and over again, and tasting again the joys of a double salary. Yet even his hardy imagination rarely rose to the height of Sally Fortune. That hour of dreaming, however, made the day of labor almost pleasant.

This time, in the very middle of his dream, he reached the cross-roads saloon and general merchandise store of Flanders; so he banished his visions with a compelling shrug of the shoulders and rode for it at a gallop, a hot dryness growing in his throat at every stride. Quick service he was sure to get, for there were not more than half a dozen cattle-ponies standing in front of the little building with its rickety walls guiltless of paint save for the one great sign inscribed with uncertain letters.

He swung from the saddle, tossed the reins over the head of the mustang, made a stride forward—and then checked himself with a soft curse and reached for his gun.

For the door of the bar dashed open and down the steps rushed a tall man with light yellow moustache, so long that it literally blew on either side over his shoulders as he ran; in either hand he carried a revolver—a two-gun man, fleeing, perhaps, from another murder.

For Nash recognized in him a character notorious through a thousand miles of the range, Sandy Ferguson, nicknamed by the color of that famous moustache, which was envied and dreaded so far and so wide. It was not fear that made Nash halt, for otherwise he would have finished the motion and whipped out his gun; but at least it was something closely akin to fear.

For that matter, there were unmistakable signs in Sandy himself of what would have been called arrant terror in any other man. His face was so bloodless that the pallor showed even through the leathery tan; one eye stared wildly, the other being sheltered under a clumsy patch which could not quite conceal the ugly bruise beneath. Under his great moustache his lips were as puffed and swollen as the lips of a Negro.

Staggering in his haste, he whirled a few paces from the house and turned, his guns levelled. At the same moment the door opened and the perspiring figure of little fat Flanders appeared. Scorn and anger rather than hate or any bloodlust appeared in his face. His right arm, hanging loosely at his side, held a revolver, and he seemed to have the greatest unconcern for the leveled weapons of the gunman.

He made a gesture with that armed hand, and Sandy winced as though a whiplash had flicked him.

"Steady up, damn your eyes!" bellowed Flanders, "and put them guns away. Put 'em up; hear me?"

To the mortal astonishment of Nash, Sandy obeyed, keeping the while a fascinated eye upon the little Dutchman.

"Now climb your hoss and beat it, and if I ever find you in reach again, I'll send my kid out to rope you and give you a hoss-whippin'."

The gun fighter lost no time. A single leap carried him into his saddle and he was off over the sand with a sharp rattle of the beating hoofs.

"Well," breathed Nash, "I'll be hanged."

"Sure you will," suggested Flanders, at once changing his frown for a smile of somewhat professional good nature, as one who greeted an old customer, "sure you will unless you come in an' have a drink on the house. I want something myself to forget what I been doin'. I feel like the dog-catcher."

Steve, deeply meditative, strode into the room.

"Partner," he said gravely to Flanders, "I've always prided myself on having eyes a little better than the next one, but just now I guess I must have been seein' double. Seemed to me that that was Sandy Ferguson that you hot-footed out of that door—or has Sandy got a double?"

"Nope," said the bartender, wiping the last of the perspiration from his forehead, "that's Sandy, all right."

"Then gimme a big drink. I need it."

The bottle spun expertly across the bar, and the glasses tinkled after.

"Funny about him, all right," nodded Flanders, "but then it's happened the same way with others I could tell about. As long as he was winnin' Sandy was the king of any roost. The minute he lost a fight he wasn't worth so many pounds of salt pork. Take a hoss; a fine hoss is often jest the same. Long as it wins nothin' can touch some of them blooded boys. But let 'em go under the wire second, maybe jest because they's packing twenty pounds too much weight, and they're never any good any more. Any second-rather can lick 'em. I lost five hundred iron boys on a hoss that laid down like that."

"All of which means," suggested Nash, "that Sandy has been licked?"

"Licked? No, he ain't been licked, but he's been plumb annihilated, washed off the map, cleaned out, faded, rubbed into the dirt; if there was some stronger way of puttin' it, I would. Only last night, at that, but now look at him. A girl that never seen a man before could tell that he wasn't any more dangerous now than if he was made of putty; but if the fool keeps packin' them guns he's sure to get into trouble."

He raised his glass.

"So here's to the man that Sandy was and ain't no more."

They drank solemnly.

"Maybe you took the fall out of him yourself, Flanders?"

"Nope. I ain't no fighter, Steve. You know that. The feller that downed Sandy was—a tenderfoot. Yep, a greenhorn."

"Ah-h-h," drawled Nash softly, "I thought so."

"You did?"

"Anyway, let's hear the story. Another drink—on me, Flanders."

"It was like this. Along about evening of yesterday Sandy was in here with a couple of other boys. He was pretty well lighted—the glow was circulatin' promiscuous, in fact—when in comes a feller about your height, Steve, but lighter. Good lookin', thin face, big dark eyes like a girl. He carried the signs of a long ride on him. Well, sir, he walks up to the bar and says: 'Can you make me a very sour lemonade, Mr. Bartender?'

"I grabbed the edge of the bar and hung on tight.

"'A which?' says I.

"'Lemonade, if you please.'

"I rolled an eye at Sandy, who was standin' there with his jaw falling, and then I got busy with lemons and the squeezer, but pretty soon Ferguson walks up to the stranger.

"'Are you English?' he asks.

"I knew by his tone what was comin', so I slid the gun I keep behind the bar closer and got prepared for a lot of damaged crockery.

"'I?' says the tenderfoot. 'Why, no. What makes you ask?'

"'Your damned funny way of talkin',' says Sandy.

"'Oh,' says the greenhorn, nodding as if he was thinkin' this over and discovering a little truth in it. 'I suppose the way I talk is a little unusual.'

"'A little rotten,' says Sandy. 'Did I hear you askin' for a lemonade?'

"'You did.'

"'Would I seem to be askin' too many questions,' says Sandy, terrible polite, 'if I inquires if bar whisky ain't good enough for you?'

"The tenderfoot, he stands there jest as easy as you an' me stand here now, and he laughed.

"He says: 'The bar whisky I've tasted around this country is not very good for any one, unless, perhaps, after a snake has bitten you. Then it works on the principle of poison fight poison, eh?'

"Sandy says after a minute: 'I'm the most quietest, gentle, innercent cowpuncher that ever rode the range, but I'd tell a man that it riles me to hear good bar whisky insulted like this. Look at me! Do I look as if whisky ain't good for a man?'

"'Why,' says the tenderfoot, 'you look sort of funny to me.'

"He said it as easy as if he was passin' the morning with Ferguson, but I seen that it was the last straw with Sandy. He hefted out both guns and trained 'em on the greenhorn.

"I yelled: 'Sandy, for God's sake, don't be killin' a tenderfoot!'

"'If whisky will kill him he's goin' to die,' says Sandy. 'Flanders, pour out a drink of rye for this gent.'

"I did it, though my hand was shaking a lot, and the chap takes the glass and raises it polite, and looks at the color of it. I thought he was goin' to drink, and starts wipin' the sweat off'n my forehead.

"But this chap, he sets down the glass and smiles over to Sandy.

"'Listen,' he says, still grinnin', 'in the old days I suppose this would have been a pretty bluff, but it won't work with me now. You want me to drink this glass of very bad whisky, but I'm sure that you don't want it badly enough to shoot me.

"'There are many reasons. In the old days a man shot down another and then rode off on his horse and was forgotten, but in these days the telegraph is faster than any horse that was ever foaled. They'd be sure to get you, sir, though you might dodge them for a while. And I believe that for a crime such as you threaten, they have recently installed a little electric chair which is a perfectly good inducer of sleep—in fact, it is better than a cradle. Taking these things all into consideration, I take it for granted that you are bluffing, my friend, and one of my favorite occupations is calling a bluff. You look dangerous, but I've an idea that you are as yellow as your moustache.'

"Sandy, he sort of swelled up all over like a poisoned dog.

"He says: 'I begin to see your style. You want a clean man-handlin', which suits me uncommon well.'

"With that, he lays down his guns, soft and careful, and puts up his fists, and goes for the other gent.

"He makes his pass, which should have sent the other gent into kingdom come. But it didn't. No, sir, the tenderfoot, he seemed to evaporate. He wasn't there when the fist of Ferguson come along. Ferguson, he checked up short and wheeled around and charged again like a bull. And he missed again. And so they kept on playin' a sort of a game of tag over the place, the stranger jest side-steppin' like a prize-fighter, the prettiest you ever seen, and not developin' when Sandy started on one of his swings.

"At last one of Sandy's fists grazed him on the shoulder and sort of peeved him, it looked like. He ducks under Sandy's next punch, steps in, and wallops Sandy over the eye—that punch didn't travel more'n six inches. But it slammed Sandy down in a corner like he's been shot.

"He was too surprised to be much hurt, though, and drags himself up to his feet, makin' a pass at his pocket at the same time. Then he came again, silent and thinkin' of blood, I s'pose, with a knife in his hand.

"This time the tenderfoot didn't wait. He went in with a sort of hitch step, like a dancer. Ferguson's knife carved the air beside the tenderfoot's head, and then the skinny boy jerked up his right and his left—one, two—into Sandy's mouth. Down he goes again—slumps down as if all the bones in his body was busted—right down on his face. The other feller grabs his shoulder and jerks him over on his back.

"He stands lookin' down at him for a moment, and then he says, sort of thoughtful: 'He isn't badly hurt, but I suppose I shouldn't have hit him twice.'

"Can you beat that, Steve? You can't!

"When Sandy come to he got up to his feet, wobbling—seen his guns—went over and scooped 'em up, with the eye of the tenderfoot on him all the time—scooped 'em up—stood with 'em all poised—and so he backed out through the door. It wasn't any pretty thing to see. The tenderfoot, he turned to the bar again.

"'If you don't mind,' he says, 'I think I'll switch my order and take that whisky instead. I seem to need it.'

"'Son!' says I, 'there ain't nothin' in the house you can't have for the askin'. Try some of this!'

"And I pulled out a bottle of my private stock—you know the stuff; I've had it twenty-five years, and it was ten years old when I got it. That ain't as much of a lie as it sounds.

"He takes a glass of it and sips it, sort of suspicious, like a wolf scentin' the wind for an elk in winter. Then his face lighted up like a lantern had been flashed on it. You'd of thought that he was lookin' his long-lost brother in the eye from the way he smiled at me. He holds the glass up and lets the light come through it, showin' the little traces and bubbles of oil.

"'May I know your name?' he says.

"It made me feel like Rockerbilt, hearin' him say that, in *that* special voice.

"'Me,' says I, 'I'm Flanders.'

"'It's an honor to know you, Mr. Flanders,' he says. 'My name is Anthony Bard.'

"We shook hands, and his grip was three fourths man, I'll tell the world.

"'Good liquor,' says he, 'is like a fine lady. Only a gentleman can appreciate it. I drink to you, sir.'

"So that's how Sandy Ferguson went under the sod. To-day? Well, I couldn't let Ferguson stand in a barroom where a gentleman had been, could I?"

* * *

Even the stout roan grew weary during the third day, and when they topped the last rise of hills, and looked down to darker shadows in Eldara in the black heart of the hollow, the mustang stood with hanging head, and one ear flopped forward. Cruel indeed had been the pace which Nash maintained, yet they had never been able to overhaul the flying piebald of Anthony Bard.

As they trotted down the slope, Nash looked to his equipment, handled his revolver, felt the strands of the lariat, and resting only his toes in the stirrups, eased all his muscles to make sure that they were uncramped from the long journey. He was fit; there was no doubt of that.

Coming down the main street—for Eldara boasted no fewer than three thoroughfares—the first houses which Nash passed showed no lights. As far as he could see, the blinds were all drawn; not even the glimmer of a candle showed, and the voices which he heard were muffled and low.

He thought of plague or some other disaster which might have overtaken the little village and wiped out nine tenths of the populace in a day. Only such a thing could account for silence in Eldara. There should have been bursts and roars of laughter here and there, and now and then a harsh stream of cursing. There should have been clatter of kitchen tins; there should have been neighing of horses; there should have been the quiver and tingle of children's voices at play in the dusty streets. But there was none of this. The silence was as thick and oppressive as the unbroken dark of the night. Even Butler's saloon was closed!

This, however, was something which he would not believe, no matter what testimony his eyes gave him. He rode up to a shuttered window and kicked it with his heel.

Only the echoes of that racket replied to him from the interior of the place. He swore, somewhat touched with awe, and kicked again.

A faint voice called: "Who's there?"

"Steve Nash. What the devil's happened to Eldara?"

The boards of the shutter stirred, opened, so that the man within could look out.

"Is it Steve, honest?"

"Damn it, Butler, don't you know my voice? What's turned Eldara into a cemetery?"

"Cemetery's right. 'Butch' Conklin and his gang are going to raid the place to-night."

"Butch Conklin?"

And Nash whistled long and low.

"But why the devil don't the boys get together if they know Butch is coming with his gunmen?"

"That's what they've done. Every able-bodied man in town is out in the hills trying to surprise Conklin's gang before they hit town with their guns going."

Butler was a one-legged man, so Nash kept back the question which naturally formed in his mind.

"How do they know Conklin is coming? Who gave the tip?"

"Conklin himself."

"What? Has he been in town?"

"Right. Came in roaring drunk."

"Why'd they let him get away again?"

"Because the sheriff's a bonehead and because our marshal is solid ivory. That's why."

"What happened?"

"Butch came in drunk, as I was saying, which he generally is, but he wasn't giving no trouble at all, and nobody felt particular called on to cross him and ask questions. He was real sociable, in fact, and that's how the mess was started."

"Go on. I don't get your drift."

"Everybody was treatin' Butch like he was the king of the earth and not passin' out any backtalk, all except one tenderfoot——"

But here a stream of tremendous profanity burst from Nash. It rose, it rushed on, it seemed an exhaustless vocabulary built up by long practice on mustangs and cattle.

At length: "Is that damned fool in Eldara?"

"D'you know him?"

"No. Anyway, go on. What happened?"

"I was sayin' that Butch was feelin' pretty sociable. It went all right in the bars. He was in here and didn't do nothin' wrong. Even paid for all the drinks for everybody in the house, which nobody could ask more even from a white man. But then Butch got hungry and went up the street to Sally Fortune's place."

A snarl came from Nash.

"Did they let that swine go in there?"

"Who'd stop him? Would you?"

"I'd try my damnedest."

"Anyway, in he went and got the center table and called for ten dollars' worth of bacon and eggs—which there hasn't been an egg in Eldara this week. Sally, she told him, not being afraid even of Butch. He got pretty sore at that and said that it was a frame-up and everyone was ag'in' him. But finally he allowed that if she'd sit down to the table and keep him company he'd manage to make out on whatever her cook had ready to eat.

"And Sally done it?" groaned Nash.

"Sure; it was like a dare—and you know Sally. She'd risk her whole place any time for the sake of a bet."

"I know it, but don't rub it in."

"She fetched out a steak and served Butch as if he'd been a king and then sat down beside him and started kiddin' him along, with all the gang of us sittin' or standin' around and laughin' fit to bust, but not loud for fear Butch would get annoyed.

"Then two things come in together and spoiled the prettiest little party that was ever started in Eldara. First was that player piano which Sally got shipped in and paid God-knows-how-much for; the second was this greenhorn I was tellin' you about."

"Go on," said Nash, the little snarl coming back in his voice. "Tell me how the tenderfoot walked up and kicked Butch out of the place."

"Somebody been tellin' you?"

"No; I just been readin' the mind of Eldara."

"It was a nice play, though. This Bard—we found out later that was his name—walks in, takes a table, and not being served none too quick, he walks over and slips a nickel in the slot of the piano. Out she starts with a piece of rippin' ragtime—you know how loud it plays? Butch, he kept on talkin' for a minute, but couldn't hear himself think. Finally he bellers: 'Who turned that damned tin-pan loose?'

"This Bard walks up and bows. He says: 'Sir, I came here to find food, and since I can't get service, I'll take music as a substitute.'

"Them was the words he used, Steve, honest to God. Used them to Butch!

"Well, Conklin was too flabbergasted to budge, and Bard, he leaned over and says to Sally: 'This floor is fairly smooth. Suppose you and I dance till I get a chance to eat?'

"We didn't know whether to laugh or to cheer, but most of us compromised by keeping an eye on Butch's gun.

"Sally says, 'Sure I'll dance,' and gets up.

"'Wait!' hollers Butch; 'are you leavin' me for this wall-eyed galoot?'

"There ain't nothin' Sally loves more'n a fight—we all know that. But this time I guess she took pity on the poor tenderfoot, or maybe she jest didn't want to get her floor all messed up.

"'Keep your hat on, Butch,' she says, 'all I want to do is to give him some motherly advice.'

"'If you're acting that part,' says Bard, calm as you please, 'I've got to tell mother that she's been keeping some pretty bad company.'

"'Some what?' bellers Butch, not believin' his ears.

"And young Bard, he steps around the girl and stands over Butch.

"'Bad company is what I said,' he repeats, 'but maybe I can be convinced.'

"'Easy,' says Butch, and reaches for his gun.

"We all dived for the door, but me being held up on account of my missing leg, I was slow an' couldn't help seein' what happened. Butch was fast, but the young feller was faster. He had Butch by the wrist before the gun came clear—just gave a little twist—and there he stood with the gun in his hand pointin' into Butch's face, and Butch sittin' there like a feller in a trance or wakin' up out of a bad dream.

"Then he gets up, slow and dignified, though he had enough liquor in him to float a ship.

"'I been mobbed,' he says, 'it's easy to see that. I come here peaceful and quiet, and here I been mobbed. But I'm comin' back, boys, and I ain't comin' alone.'

"There was our chance to get him, while he was walking out of that place without a gun, but somehow nobody moved for him. He didn't look none too easy, even without his shootin' irons. Out he goes into the night, and we stood around starin' at each other. Everybody was upset, except Sally and Bard.

"He says: 'Miss Fortune, this is our dance, I think.'

"'Excuse me,' says Sally, 'I almost forgot about it.'

"And they started to dance to the piano, waltzin' around among the tables; the rest of us lit out for home because we knew that Butch would be on his way with his gang before we got very far under cover. But hey, Steve, where you goin'?"

"I'm going to get in on that dance," called Nash, and was gone at a racing gallop down the street.

CHAPTER TEN

THE ROUNDUP

Theodore Roosevelt

During the winter-time there is ordinarily but little work done among the cattle. There is some line riding, and a continual lookout is kept for the very weak animals,—usually cows and calves, who have to be driven in, fed, and housed; but most of the stock are left to shift for themselves, undisturbed. Almost every stock-growers' association forbids branding any calves before the spring round-up. If great bands of cattle wander off the range, parties may be fitted out to go after them and bring them back; but this is only done when absolutely necessary, as when the drift of the cattle has been towards an Indian reservation or a settled granger country, for the weather is very severe, and the horses are so poor that their food must be carried along.

The bulk of the work is done during the summer, including the late spring and early fall, and consists mainly in a succession of round-ups, beginning, with us, in May and ending towards the last of October.

But a good deal may be done in the intervals by riding over one's range. Frequently, too, herding will be practiced on a large scale.

Still more important is the "trail" work: cattle, while driven from one range to another, or to a shipping point for beef, being said to be "on the trail." For years, the over-supply from the vast breeding ranches to the south, especially in Texas, has been driven northward in large herds, either to the shipping towns along the great railroads, or else to the fattening ranges of the North-west; it having been found, so far, that while the calf crop is larger in the South, beeves become much heavier in the North. Such cattle, for the most part, went along tolerably well-marked routes or trails, which became for the time being of great importance, flourishing—and extremely lawless—towns growing up along them; but with the growth of the railroad system, and above all with the filling-up of the northern ranges, these trails have steadily become of less and less consequence, though many herds still travel them on their way to the already crowded ranges of western Dakota and Montana, or to the Canadian regions beyond. The trail work is something by itself. The herds may be on the trail several months, averaging fifteen miles or less a day. The cowboys accompanying each have to undergo much hard toil, of a peculiarly same and wearisome kind, on account of the extreme slowness with which everything must be done, as trail cattle should never be hurried. The foreman of a trail outfit must be not only a veteran cowhand, but also a miracle of patience and resolution.

Round-up work is far less irksome, there being an immense amount of dash and excitement connected with it; and when once the cattle are on the range, the important work is done during the round-up. On cow ranches, or wherever there is breeding stock, the spring round-up is the great event of the season, as it is then that the bulk of the calves are branded. It usually lasts six weeks, or thereabouts; but its end by no means implies rest for the stockman. On the contrary, as soon as it is over, wagons are sent to work out-of-the-way parts of the country that have been passed over, but where cattle are supposed to have drifted; and by the time these have come back the first beef round-up has begun, and thereafter beeves are steadily gathered and shipped, at least from among the larger herds, until cold weather sets in; and in the fall there is another round-up, to brand the late calves and see that the stock is got back on the range. As all of these round-ups are of one character, a description of the most important, taking place in the spring, will be enough.

In April we begin to get up the horses. Throughout the winter very few have been kept for use, as they are then poor and weak, and must be given grain and hay if they are to be worked. The men in the line camps need two or three apiece, and each man at the home ranch has a couple more; but the rest are left out to shift for themselves, which the tough, hardy little fellows are well able to do. Ponies can pick up a living where cattle die; though the scanty feed, which they may have to uncover by pawing off the snow, and the bitter weather often make them look very gaunt by spring-time. But the first warm rains bring up the green grass, and then all the live-stock gain flesh with wonderful rapidity. When the spring round-up begins the horses should be as fat and sleek as possible. After running all winter free, even the most sober pony is apt to betray an inclination to buck; and, if possible, we like to ride every animal once or twice before we begin to do real work with him. Animals that have escaped for any length of time are almost as bad to handle as if they had never been broken. One of the two horses mentioned in a former chapter as having been gone eighteen months has, since his return, been suggestively dubbed "Dynamite Jimmy," on account of the incessant and eruptive energy with which he bucks. Many of our horses, by the way, are thus named from some feat or peculiarity. Wire Fence, when being broken, ran into one of the abominations after which he is now called; Hackamore once got away and remained out for three weeks with a hackamore, or breaking-halter, on him; Macaulay contracted the habit of regularly getting rid of the huge Scotchman to whom he was intrusted; Bulberry Johnny spent the hour or two after he was first mounted in a large patch of thorny bulberry bushes, his distracted rider unable to get him to do anything but move round sidewise in a circle; Fall Back would never get to the front; Water Skip always jumps mud-puddles; and there are a dozen others with names as purely descriptive.

The stock-growers of Montana, of the western part of Dakota, and even of portions of extreme northern Wyoming,—that is, of all the grazing lands lying in the basin of the Upper Missouri,—have united, and formed themselves into the great Montana Stockgrowers' Association. Among the countless benefits they have derived from this course, not the least has been the way in which the various round-ups work in with and supplement one another. At the spring meeting of the association, the entire territory mentioned above, including perhaps a hundred thousand square miles, is mapped out into round-up districts, which generally are changed but slightly from year to year, and the times and places for the round-ups to begin refixed so that those of adjacent districts may be run with a view to the best interests of all. Thus the stockmen along the Yellowstone have one round-up; we along the Little Missouri have another; and the country lying between, through which the Big Beaver flows, is almost equally important to both. Accordingly, one spring, the Little Missouri round-up, beginning May 25, and working down-stream, was timed so as to reach the mouth of the Big Beaver about June 1, the Yellowstone round-up beginning at that date and place. Both then worked up the Beaver together to its head, when the Yellowstone men turned to the west and we bent back to our own river; thus the bulk of the strayed cattle of each were brought back to their respective ranges. Our own round-up district covers the Big and Little Beaver creeks, which rise near each other, but empty into the Little Missouri nearly a hundred and fifty miles apart, and so much of the latter river as lies between their mouths.

The captain or foreman of the round-up, upon whom very much of its efficiency and success depends, is chosen beforehand. He is, of course, an expert cowman, thoroughly acquainted with the country; and he must also be able to command and to keep control of the wild rough-riders he has under him—a feat needing both tact and firmness.

At the appointed day all meet at the place from which the round-up is to start. Each ranch, of course, has most work to be done in its own round-up district, but it is also necessary to have representatives in all those surrounding it. A large outfit may employ a dozen cowboys, or over, in the home district, and yet have nearly as many more representing its interest in the various ones adjoining. Smaller outfits generally club together to run a wagon and send outside representatives, or else go along with their stronger neighbors, they paying part of the expenses. A large outfit, with a herd of twenty thousand cattle or more, can, if necessary, run a round-up entirely by itself, and is able to act independently of outside help; it is therefore at a great advantage compared with those that can take no step effectively without their neighbors' consent and assistance.

If the starting-point is some distance off, it may be necessary to leave home three or four days in advance. Before this we have got everything in readiness; have overhauled the wagons, shod any horse whose forefeet are tender,—as a rule, all our ponies go barefooted,—and left things in order at the ranch. Our outfit may be taken as a sample of every one else's. We have a stout four-horse wagon to carry the bedding and the food; in its rear a mess-chest is rigged to hold the knives, forks, cans, etc. All our four team-horses are strong, willing animals, though of no great size, being originally just "broncos," or unbroken native horses, like the others. The teamster is also cook: a man who is a really first-hand at both driving and cooking—and our present teamster is both—can always command his price. Besides our own men, some cowboys from neighboring ranches and two or three representatives from other round-up districts are always along, and we generally have at least a dozen "riders," as they are termed,—that is, cowboys, or "cowpunchers," who do the actual cattle-work,—with the wagon. Each of these has a string of eight or ten ponies; and to take charge of the saddle-band, thus consisting of a hundred odd head, there are two herders, always known as "horse-wranglers"—one for the day and one for the night. Occasionally there will be two wagons, one to carry the bedding and one the food, known, respectively, as the bed and the mess wagon; but this is not usual.

While traveling to the meeting point the pace is always slow, as it is an object to bring the horses on the ground as fresh as possible. Accordingly we keep at a walk almost all day, and the riders, having nothing else to do, assist the wranglers in driving the saddle-band, three or four going in front, and others on the side, so that the horses shall keep on a walk. There is always some trouble with the animals at the starting out, as they are very fresh and are restive under the saddle. The herd is likely to stampede, and any beast that is frisky or vicious is sure to show its worst side. To do really effective cow-work a pony should be well broken; but many even of the old ones have vicious traits, and almost every man will have in his string one or two young horses, or broncos, hardly broken at all. Thanks to the rough methods of breaking in vogue on the plains many even of the so called broken animals retain always certain bad habits, the most common being that of bucking. Of the sixty odd horses on my ranch all but half a dozen were broken by ourselves; and though my men are all good riders, yet a good rider is not necessarily a good horse-breaker, and indeed it was an absolute impossibility properly to break so many animals in the short time at our command—for we had to use them almost immediately after they were bought. In consequence, very many of my horses have to this day traits not likely to set a timid or a clumsy rider at his ease. One or two run away and cannot be held by even the strongest bit; others can hardly be bridled or saddled until they have been thrown; two or three have a tendency to fall over backward; and half of them buck more or less, some so hard that only an expert can sit them; several I never ride myself, save from dire necessity.

In riding these wild, vicious horses, and in careering over such very bad ground, especially at night, accidents are always occurring. A man who is merely an ordinary rider is certain to have a pretty hard time. On my first round-up I had a string of nine horses, four of them broncos, only broken to the extent of having each been saddled once or twice. One of them it was an impossibility to bridle or to saddle single-handed; it was very difficult to get on or off him, and he was exceedingly nervous if a man moved his hands or feet; but he had no bad tricks. The second soon became perfectly quiet. The third turned out to be one of the worst buckers on the ranch: once, when he bucked me off, I managed to fall on a stone and broke a rib. The fourth had a still worse habit, for he would balk and then throw himself over backward: once, when I was not quick enough, he caught me and broke something in the point of my shoulder, so that it was some weeks before I could raise the arm freely. My hurts were far from serious, and did not interfere with my riding and working as usual through the round-up; but I was heartily glad when it ended, and ever since have religiously done my best to get none but gentle horses in my own string. However, every one gets falls from or with his horse now and then in the cow country; and even my men, good riders though they are, are sometimes injured. One of them once broke his ankle; another a rib; another was on one occasion stunned, remaining unconscious for some hours; and yet another had certain of his horses buck under him so hard and long as finally to hurt his lungs and make him cough blood. Fatal accidents occur annually in almost every district, especially if there is much work to be done among stampeded cattle at night; but on my own ranch none of my men have ever been seriously hurt, though on one occasion a cowboy from another ranch, who was with my wagon, was killed, his horse falling and pitching him heavily on his head.

For bedding, each man has two or three pairs of blankets, and a tarpaulin or small wagon-sheet. Usually, two or three sleep together. Even in June the nights are generally cool and pleasant, and it is chilly in the early mornings; although this is not always so, and when the weather stays hot and mosquitoes are plenty, the hours of darkness, even in midsummer, seem painfully long. In the Bad Lands proper we are not often bothered very seriously by these winged pests; but in the low bottoms of the big Missouri, and beside many of the reedy ponds and great sloughs out on the prairie, they are a perfect scourge. During the very hot nights, when they are especially active, the bed-clothes make a man feel absolutely smothered, and yet his only chance for sleep is to wrap himself tightly up, head and all; and even then some of the pests will usually force their way in. At sunset I have seen the mosquitoes rise up from the land like a dense cloud, to make the hot, stifling night one long torture; the horses would neither lie down nor graze, traveling restlessly to and fro till daybreak, their bodies streaked and bloody, and the insects settling on them so as to make them all one color, a uniform gray; while the men, after a few hours' tossing about in the vain attempt to sleep, rose, built a little fire of damp sage brush, and thus endured the misery as best they could until it was light enough to work.

But if the weather is fine, a man will never sleep better nor more pleasantly than in the open air after a hard day's work on the round-up; nor will an ordinary shower or gust of wind disturb him in the least, for he simply draws the tarpaulin over his head and goes on sleeping. But now and then we have a wind-storm that might better be called a whirlwind and has to be met very differently; and two or three days or nights of rain insure the wetting of the blankets, and therefore shivering discomfort on the part of the would-be sleeper. For two or three hours all goes well; and it is rather soothing to listen to the steady patter of the great raindrops on the canvas. But then it will be found that a corner has been left open through which the water can get in, or else the tarpaulin will begin to leak somewhere; or perhaps the water will have collected in a hollow underneath and have begun to soak through. Soon a little stream trickles in, and every effort to remedy matters merely results in a change for the worse. To move out of the way ensures getting wet in a fresh spot; and the best course is to lie still and accept the evils that have come with what fortitude one can. Even thus, the first night a man can sleep pretty well; but if the rain continues, the second night, when the blankets are already damp, and when the water comes through more easily, is apt to be most unpleasant.

Of course, a man can take little spare clothing on a round-up; at the very outside two or three clean handkerchiefs, a pair of socks, a change of underclothes, and the most primitive kind of washing-apparatus, all wrapped up in a stout jacket which is to be worn when night herding. The inevitable "slicker," or oil-skin coat, which gives complete protection from the wet, is always carried behind the saddle.

At the meeting-place there is usually a delay of a day or two to let everyone come in; and the plain on which the encampment is made becomes a scene of great bustle and turmoil. The heavy four-horse wagons jolt in from different quarters, the horse-wranglers rushing madly to and fro in the endeavor to keep the different saddle-bands from mingling, while the "riders," or cowboys, with each wagon jog along in a body. The representatives from outside districts ride in singly or by twos and threes, every man driving before him his own horses, one of them loaded with his bedding. Each wagon wheels out of the way into some camping-place not too near the others, the bedding is tossed out on the ground, and then everyone is left to do what he wishes, while the different wagon bosses, or foremen, seek out the captain of the round-up to learn what his plans are.

There is a good deal of rough but effective discipline and method in the way in which a round-up is carried on. The captain of the whole has as lieutenants the various wagon foremen, and in making demands for men to do some special service he will usually merely designate some foreman to take charge of the work and let him parcel it out among his men to suit himself. The captain of the round-up or the foreman of a wagon may himself be a ranchman; if such is not the case, and the ranchman nevertheless comes along, he works and fares precisely as do the other cowboys.

While the head men are gathered in a little knot, planning out the work, the others are dispersed over the plain in every direction, racing, breaking rough horses, or simply larking with one another. If a man has an especially bad horse, he usually takes such an opportunity, when he has plenty of time, to ride him; and while saddling he is surrounded by a crowd of most unsympathetic associates who greet with uproarious mirth any misadventure. A man on a bucking horse is always considered fair game, every squeal and jump of the bronco being hailed with cheers of delighted irony for the rider and shouts to "stay with him." The antics of a vicious bronco show infinite variety of detail, but are all modeled on one general plan. When the rope settles round his neck the fight begins, and it is only after much plunging and snorting that a twist is taken over his nose, or else a hackamore—a species of severe halter, usually made of plaited hair—slipped on his head. While being bridled he strikes viciously with his fore feet, and perhaps has to be blindfolded or thrown down; and to get the saddle on him is quite as difficult. When saddled, he may get rid of his exuberant spirits by bucking under the saddle, or may reserve all his energies for the rider. In the last case, the man keeping tight hold with his left hand of the cheek-strap, so as to prevent the horse from getting his head down until he is fairly seated, swings himself quickly into the saddle. Up rises the bronco's back into an arch; his head, the ears laid straight back, goes down between his forefeet, and, squealing savagely, he makes a succession of rapid, stiff-legged, jarring bounds. Sometimes he is a "plunging" bucker, who runs forward all the time while bucking; or he may buck steadily in one place, or "sun-fish,"—that is, bring first one shoulder down almost to the ground and then the other,—or else he may change ends while in the air. A first-class rider will sit throughout it all without moving from the saddle, quirting[1] his horse all the time, though his hat may be jarred off his head and his revolver out of its sheath. After a few jumps, however, the average man grasps hold of the horn of the

---

1 *Quirt is the name of the short flexible riding-whip used throughout cowboy land. The term is a Spanish one.*

saddle—the delighted onlookers meanwhile earnestly advising him not to "go to leather"—and is contented to get through the affair in any shape provided he can escape without being thrown off. An accident is of necessity borne with a broad grin, as any attempt to resent the raillery of the bystanders—which is perfectly good-humored—would be apt to result disastrously. Cowboys are certainly extremely good riders. As a class they have no superiors. Of course, they would at first be at a disadvantage in steeple-chasing or fox-hunting, but their average of horsemanship is without doubt higher than that of the men who take part in these latter amusements. A cowboy would learn to ride across country in a quarter of the time it would take a cross-country rider to learn to handle a vicious bronco or to do good cow-work round and in a herd.

On such a day, when there is no regular work, there will often also be horse-races, as each outfit is pretty sure to have some running pony which it believes can outpace any other. These contests are always short-distance dashes, for but a few hundred yards. Horse-racing is a mania with most plainsmen, white or red. A man with a good racing pony will travel all about with it, often winning large sums, visiting alike cow ranches, frontier towns, and Indian encampments. Sometimes the race is "pony against pony," the victor taking both steeds. In racing the men ride bareback, as there are hardly any light saddles in the cow country. There will be intense excitement and very heavy betting over a race between two well-known horses, together with a good chance of blood being shed in the attendance quarrels.

Indians and whites often race against each other as well as among themselves. I have seen several such contests, and in every case but one the white man happened to win. A race is usually run between two thick rows of spectators, on foot and on horseback, and as the racers pass, these rows close in behind them, every man yelling and shouting with all the strength of his lungs, and all waving their hats and cloaks to encourage the contestants, or firing off their revolvers and saddle guns. The little horses are fairly maddened, as is natural enough, and run as if they were crazy: were the distances longer some would be sure to drop in their tracks.

Besides the horse-races, which are, of course, the main attraction, the men at a round-up will often get up wrestling matches or footraces. In fact, everyone feels that he is off for a holiday; for after the monotony of a long winter, the cowboys look forward eagerly to the round-up, where the work is hard, it is true, but exciting and varied, and treated a good deal as a frolic. There is no eight-hour law in cowboy land: during round-up time we often count ourselves lucky if we get off with much less than sixteen hours; but the work is done in the saddle, and the men are spurred on all the time by the desire to outdo one another in feats of daring and skillful horsemanship. There is very little quarreling or fighting; and though the fun often takes the form of rather rough horse-play, yet the practice of carrying dangerous weapons makes cowboys show far more rough courtesy to each other and far less rudeness to strangers than is the case among, for instance, Eastern miners, or even lumbermen. When a quarrel may very probably result fatally, a man thinks twice before going into it: warlike people or classes always treat one another with a certain amount of consideration and politeness. The moral tone of a cow-camp, indeed, is rather high: than otherwise. Meanness, cowardice, and dishonesty are not tolerated. There is a high regard for truthfulness and keeping one's word, intense contempt for any kind of hypocrisy, and a hearty dislike for a man who shirks his work. Many of the men gamble and drink, but many do neither; and the conversation is not worse than in most bodies composed wholly of male human beings. A cowboy will not submit tamely to an insult, and is ever ready to avenge his own wrongs; nor has he an overwrought fear of shedding blood. He possesses, in fact, few of the emasculated, milk-and-water moralities admired by the pseudo-philanthropists; but he does possess, to a very high degree, the stern, manly qualities that are invaluable to a nation.

The method of work is simple. The mess-wagons and loose horses, after breaking camp in the morning, move on in a straight line for some few miles, going into camp again before midday; and the day herd, consisting of all the cattle that have been found far off their range, and which are to be brought back there, and of any others that it is necessary to gather, follows on afterwards. Meanwhile the cowboys scatter out and drive in all the cattle from the country round about, going perhaps ten or fifteen miles back from the line of march, and meeting at the place where camp has already been pitched. The wagons always keep some little distance from one another, and the saddle-bands do the same, so that the horses may not get mixed. It is rather picturesque to see the four-horse teams filing down at a trot through a pass among the buttes—the saddle-bands being driven along at a smart pace to one side or behind, the teamsters cracking their whips, and the horse-wranglers calling and shouting as they ride rapidly from side to side behind the horses, urging on the stragglers by dexterous touches with the knotted ends of their long lariats that are left trailing from the saddle. The country driven over is very rough, and it is often necessary to double up teams and put on eight horses to each wagon in going up an unusually steep pitch, or hauling through a deep mud-hole, or over a river crossing where there is quicksand.

The speed and thoroughness with which a country can be worked depends, of course, very largely upon the number of riders. Ours is probably about an average roundup as regards size. The last spring I was out, there were half a dozen wagons along; the saddle-bands numbered about a hundred each; and the morning we started, sixty men in the saddle splashed across the shallow ford of the river that divided the plain where we had camped from the valley of the long winding creek up which we were first to work.

In the morning the cook is preparing breakfast long before the first glimmer of dawn. As soon as it is ready, probably about 3 o'clock, he utters a long-drawn shout, and all the sleepers feel it is time to be up on the instant, for they know there can be no such thing as delay on the round-up, under penalty of being set afoot. Accordingly they bundle out, rubbing their eyes and yawning, draw on their boots and trousers,—if they have taken the latter off,—roll up and cord their bedding, and usually without any attempt at washing crowd over to the little smoldering fire, which is placed in a hole dug in the ground, so that there may be no risk of its spreading. The men are rarely very hungry at breakfast, and it is a meal that has to be eaten in shortest order, so it is perhaps the least important. Each man, as he comes up, grasps a tin cup and plate from the mess-box, pours out his tea or coffee, with sugar, but, of course, no milk, helps himself to one or two of the biscuits that have been baked in a Dutch oven, and perhaps also to a slice of the fat pork swimming in the grease of the frying-pan, ladles himself out some beans, if there are any, and squats down on the ground to eat his breakfast. The meal is not an elaborate one; nevertheless a man will have to hurry if he wishes to eat it before hearing the foreman sing out, "Come, boys, catch your horses"; when he must drop everything and run out to the wagon with his lariat. The night wrangler is now bringing in the saddle-band, which he has been up all night guarding. A rope corral is rigged up by stretching a rope from each wheel of one side of the wagon, making a V-shaped space, into which the saddle-horses are driven. Certain men stand around to keep them inside, while the others catch the horses: many outfits have one man to do all the roping. As soon as each has caught his horse—usually a strong, tough animal, the small, quick ponies being reserved for the work round the herd in the afternoon—the band, now in charge of the day wrangler, is turned loose, and every one saddles up as fast as possible. It still lacks some time of being sunrise, and the air has in it the peculiar chill of the early morning. When all are saddled, many of the horses bucking and dancing about, the riders from the different wagons all assemble at the one where the captain is sitting, already mounted. He waits a very short time—for laggards receive but scant mercy—before announcing the proposed camping-place and parceling out the work among those present. If, as is usually the case, the line of march is along a river or creek, he appoints some man to take a dozen others and drive down (or up) it ahead of the day herd, so that the latter will not have to travel through other cattle; the day herd itself being driven and guarded by a dozen men detached for that purpose. The rest of the riders are divided into two bands, placed under men who know the country, and start out, one on each side, to bring in every head for fifteen miles back. The captain then himself rides down to the new camping-place, so as to be there as soon as any cattle are brought in.

Meanwhile the two bands, a score of riders in each, separate and make their way in opposite directions. The leader of each tries to get such a "scatter" on his men that they will cover completely all the land gone over. This morning work is called circle riding, and is peculiarly hard in the Bad Lands on account of the remarkably broken, rugged nature of the country. The men come in on lines that tend to a common center—as if the sticks of a fan were curved. As the band goes out, the leader from time to time detaches one or two men to ride down through certain sections of the country, making the shorter, or what was called inside, circles, while he keeps on; and finally, retaining as companions the two or three whose horses are toughest, makes the longest or outside circle himself, going clear back to the divide, or whatever the point may be that marks the limit of the round-up work, and then turning and working straight to the meeting-place. Each man, of course, brings in every head of cattle he can see.

These long, swift rides in the glorious spring mornings are not soon to be forgotten. The sweet, fresh air, with a touch of sharpness thus early in the day, and the rapid motion of the fiery little horse combine to make a man's blood thrill and leap with sheer buoyant light-heartedness and eager, exultant pleasure in the boldness and freedom of the life he is leading. As we climb the steep sides of the first range of buttes, wisps of wavering mist still cling in the hollows of the valley; when we come out on the top of the first great plateau, the sun flames up over its edge, and in the level, red beams the galloping horsemen throw long fantastic shadows. Black care rarely sits behind a rider whose pace is fast enough; at any rate, not when he first feels the horse move under him.

Sometimes we trot or pace, and again we lope or gallop; the few who are to take the outside circle must needs ride both hard and fast. Although only grass-fed, the horses are tough and wiry; and, moreover, are each used but once in four days, or thereabouts, so they stand the work well. The course out lies across great grassy plateaus, along knife-like ridge crests, among winding valleys and ravines, and over acres of barren, sun-scorched buttes, that look grimly grotesque and forbidding, while in the Bad Lands the riders unhesitatingly go down and over places where it seems impossible that a horse should even stand. The line of horsemen will quarter down the side of a butte, where every pony has to drop from ledge to ledge like a goat, and will go over the shoulder of a soapstone cliff, when wet and slippery, with a series of plunges and scrambles which if unsuccessful would land horses and riders in the bottom on the cañon-like washout below. In descending a clay butte after a rain, the pony will put all four feet together and slide down to the bottom almost or quite on his haunches. In very wet weather the Bad Lands are absolutely impassable; but if the ground is not slippery, it is a remarkable place that can shake the matter-of-course confidence felt by the rider in the capacity of his steed to go anywhere.

When the men on the outside circle have reached the bound set them,—whether it is a low divide, a group of jagged hills, the edge of the rolling, limitless prairie, or the long, waste reaches of alkali and sage brush,—they turn their horses' heads and begin to work down the branches of the creeks, one or two riding down the bottom, while the others keep off to the right and the left, a little ahead and fairly high up on the side hills, so as to command as much of a view as possible. On the level or rolling prairies the cattle can be seen a long way off, and it is an easy matter to gather and drive them; but in the Bad Lands every little pocket, basin, and coulée has to be searched, every gorge or ravine entered, and the dense patches of brushwood and spindling, wind-beaten trees closely examined. All the cattle are carried on ahead down the creek; and it is curious to watch the different behavior of the different breeds. A cowboy riding off to one side of the creek, and seeing a number of long-horned Texans grazing in the branches of a set of coulées, has merely to ride across the upper ends of these, uttering the drawn-out "ei-koh-h-h," so familiar to the cattlemen, and the long-horns will stop grazing, stare fixedly at him, and then, wheeling, strike off down the coulées at a trot, tails in air, to be carried along by the center riders when they reach the main creek into which the coulées lead. Our own range cattle are not so wild, but nevertheless are easy to drive; while Eastern-raised beasts have little fear of a horseman, and merely stare stupidly at him until he rides directly towards them. Every little bunch of stock is thus collected, and all are driven along together. At the place where some large fork joins the main creek another band may be met, driven by some of the men who have left earlier in the day to take one of the shorter circles; and thus, before coming down to the bottom where the wagons are camped and where the actual "round-up" itself is to take place, this one herd may include a couple of thousand head; or, on the other hand, the longest ride may not result in the finding of a dozen animals. As soon as the riders are in, they disperse to their respective wagons to get dinner and change horses, leaving the cattle to be held by one or two of their number. If only a small number of cattle have been gathered, they will all be run into one herd; if there are many of them, however, the different herds will be held separate.

A plain where a round-up is taking place offers a picturesque sight. I well remember one such. It was on a level bottom in a bend of the river, which here made an almost semicircular sweep. The bottom was in shape a long oval, hemmed in by an unbroken line of steep bluffs so that it looked like an amphitheater. Across the faces of the dazzling

white cliffs there were sharp bands of black and red, drawn by the coal seams and the layers of burned clay: the leaves of the trees and the grass had the vivid green of spring-time. The wagons were camped among the cottonwood trees fringing the river, a thin column of smoke rising up from beside each. The horses were grazing round the outskirts, those of each wagon by themselves and kept from going too near the others by their watchful guard. In the greater circular corral, towards one end, the men were already branding calves, while the whole middle of the bottom was covered with lowing herds of cattle and shouting, galloping cowboys. Apparently there was nothing but dust, noise, and confusion; but in reality the work was proceeding all the while with the utmost rapidity and certainty.

As soon as, or even before, the last circle riders have come in and have snatched a few hasty mouthfuls to serve as their midday meal, we begin to work the herd—or herds, if the one herd would be of too unwieldy size. The animals are held in a compact bunch, most of the riders forming a ring outside, while a couple from each ranch successively look the herds through and cut out those marked with their own brand. It is difficult, in such a mass of moving beasts,—for they do not stay still, but keep weaving in and out among each other,—to find all of one's own animals: a man must have natural gifts, as well as great experience, before he becomes a good brand-reader and is able really to "clean up a herd"—that is, be sure he has left nothing of his own in it.

To do good work in cutting out from a herd, not only should the rider be a good horseman, but he should also have a skillful, thoroughly trained horse. A good cutting pony is not common, and is generally too valuable to be used anywhere but in the herd. Such an one enters thoroughly into the spirit of the thing, and finds out immediately the animal his master is after; he will then follow it closely of his own accord through every wheel and double at top speed. When looking through the herd, it is necessary to move slowly; and when any animal is found it is taken to the outskirts at a walk, so as not to alarm the others. Once at the outside, however, the cowboy has to ride like lightning; for as soon as the beast he is after finds itself separated from its companions it endeavors to break back among them, and a young, range-raised steer or heifer runs like a deer. In cuffing out a cow and a calf two men have to work together. As the animals of a brand are cut out they are received and held apart by some rider detailed for the purpose, who is said to be "holding the cut."

All this time the men holding the herd have their hands full, for some animal is continually trying to break out, when the nearest man flies at it at once and after a smart chase brings it back to its fellows. As soon as all the cows, calves, and whatever else is being gathered have been cut out, the rest are driven clear off the ground and turned loose, being headed in the direction contrary to that in which we travel the following day. Then the riders surround the next herd, the men holding cuts move them up near it, and the work is begun anew.

If it is necessary to throw an animal, either to examine a brand or for any other reason, half a dozen men will have their ropes down at once; and then it is spur and quirt in the rivalry to see which can outdo the other until the beast is roped and thrown. A first-class hand will, unaided, rope, throw, and tie down a cow or steer in wonderfully short time; one of the favorite tests of competitive skill among the cowboys is the speed with which this feat can be accomplished. Usually, however, one man ropes the animal by the head and another at the same time gets the loop of his lariat over one or both its hind legs, when it is twisted over and stretched out in a second. In following an animal on horseback the man keeps steadily swinging the rope round his head, by a dexterous motion of the wrist only, until he gets a chance to throw it; when on foot, especially if catching horses in a corral, the loop is allowed to drag loosely on the ground. A good roper will hurl out the coil with marvelous accuracy and force; it fairly whistles through the air, and settles round the object with almost infallible certainty. Mexicans make the best ropers; but some Texans are very little behind them. A good horse takes as much interest in the work as does his rider, and the instant the noose settles over the victim wheels and braces himself to meet the shock, standing with his legs firmly planted, the steer or cow being thrown with a jerk. An unskillful rider and untrained horse will often themselves be thrown when the strain comes.

Sometimes an animal—usually a cow or steer, but, strangely enough, very rarely a bull—will get fighting mad, and turn on the men. If on the drive, such a beast usually is simply dropped out; but if they have time, nothing delights the cowboys more than an encounter of this sort, and the charging brute is roped and tied down in short order. Often such an one will make a very vicious fight, and is most dangerous. Once a fighting cow kept several of us busy for nearly an hour; she gored two ponies, one of them, which was luckily, hurt but slightly, being my own pet cutting horse. If a steer is hauled out of a mud-hole, its first act is usually to charge the rescuer.

As soon as all the brands of cattle are worked, and the animals that are to be driven along have been put in the day herd, attention is turned to the cows and calves, which are already gathered in different bands, consisting each of all the cows of a certain brand and all the calves that are following them. If there is a corral, each band is in turn driven into it; if there is none, a ring of riders does duty in its place. A fire is built, the irons heated, and a dozen men dismount to, as it is called, "wrestle" the calves. The best two ropers go in on their horses to catch the latter; one man keeps tally, a couple put on the brands, and the others seize, throw, and hold the little unfortunates, A first-class roper invariably catches the calf by both hind feet, and then, having taken a twist with his lariat round the horn of the saddle, drags the bawling little creature, extended at full-length, up to the fire, where it is held before it can make a struggle. A less skillful roper catches round the neck, and then, if the calf is a large one, the one who seizes it has his hands full, as the bleating, bucking animal develops astonishing strength, cuts the wildest capers, and resists frantically and with all its power. If there are seventy or eighty calves in a corral, the scene is one of the greatest confusion. The ropers, spurring and checking the fierce little horses, drag the calves up so quickly that a dozen men can hardly hold them; the men with the irons, blackened with soot, run to and fro; the calf-wrestlers, grimy with blood, dust, and sweat, work like beavers; while with the voice of a stentor the tallyman shouts out the number and sex of each calf. The dust rises in clouds, and the shouts, cheers, curses, and laughter of the men unite with the lowing of the cows and the frantic bleating of the roped calves to make a perfect babel. Now and then an old cow turns vicious and puts every one out of the corral. Or a *maverick* bull,—that is, an unbranded bull,—a yearling or a two-years-old, is caught, thrown, and branded; when he is let up there is sure to be a fine scatter. Down goes his head, and he bolts at the nearest man, who makes out of the way at top speed, amidst roars of laughter from all of his companions; while the men holding down calves swear savagely as they dodge charging mavericks, trampling horses, and taut lariats with frantic, plunging little beasts at the farther ends.

Every morning certain riders are detached to drive and to guard the day herd, which is most monotonous work, the men being on from 4 in the morning till 8 in the evening, the only rest coming at dinner-time, when they change horses. When the herd has reached the camping ground there is nothing to do but to loll listlessly over the saddle-bow in the blazing sun watching the cattle feed and sleep, and seeing that they do not spread out too much. Plodding slowly along on the trail through the columns of dust stirred up by the hoofs is not much better. Cattle travel best and fastest strung out in long lines; the swiftest taking the lead in single file, while the weak and the lazy, the young calves and the poor cows, crowd together in the rear. Two men travel along with the leaders, one on each side, to point them in the right direction; one or two others keep by the flanks, and the rest are in the rear to act as "drag-drivers" and hurry up the phalanx of reluctant weaklings. If the foremost of the string travels too fast, one rider will go along on the trail a few rods ahead, and thus keep them back so that those in the rear will not be left behind.

Generally all this is very tame and irksome; but by fits and starts there will be little flurries of excitement. Two or three of the circle riders may unexpectedly come over a butte nearby with a bunch of cattle, which at once start for the day herd, and then there will be a few minutes' furious riding hither and thither to keep them out. Or the cattle may begin to run, and then get "milling"—that is, all crowd together into a mass like a ball, wherein they move round and round, trying to keep their heads towards the center, and refusing to leave it. The only way to start them is to force one's horse in among them and cut out some of their number, which then begin to travel off by themselves, when the others will probably follow. But in spite of occasional incidents of this kind, day-herding has a dreary sameness about it that makes the men dislike and seek to avoid it.

From 8 in the evening till 4 in the morning the day herd becomes a night herd. Each wagon in succession undertakes to guard it for a night, dividing the time into watches of two hours apiece, a couple of riders taking each watch. This is generally chilly and tedious; but at times it is accompanied by intense excitement and danger, when the cattle become stampeded, whether by storm or otherwise. The first and the last watches are those chosen by preference; the others are disagreeable, the men having to turn out cold and sleepy, in the pitchy darkness, the two hours of chilly wakefulness completely breaking the night's rest. The first guards have to bed the cattle down, though the day-herders often do this themselves; it simply consists in hemming them into as small a space as possible, and then riding round them until they lie down and fall asleep. Often, especially at first, this takes some time—the beasts will keep rising and lying down again. When at last most become quiet, some perverse brute of a steer will deliberately hook them all up; they keep moving in and out among one another, and long strings of animals suddenly start out from the herd at a stretching walk, and are turned back by the nearest cowboy only to break forth at a new spot. When finally they have lain down and are chewing their cud or slumbering, the two night guards begin riding round them in opposite ways, often, on very dark nights, calling or singing to them, as the sound of the human voice on such occasions seems to have a tendency to quiet them. In inky black weather, especially when rainy, it is both difficult and unpleasant work; the main trust must be placed in the horse, which, if old at the business, will of its own accord keep pacing steadily round the herd, and head off any animals that, unseen by the rider's eyes in the darkness, are trying to break out. Usually the watch passes off without incident, but on rare occasions the cattle become restless and prone to stampede. Anything may then start them—the plunge of a horse, the sudden approach of a coyote, or the arrival of some outside steers or cows that have smelt them and come up. Every animal in the herd will be on its feet in an instant, as if by an electric shock, and off with a rush, horns and tail up. Then, no matter how rough the ground nor how pitchy black the night, the cowboys must ride for all there is in them and spare neither their own nor their horses' necks. Perhaps their charges break away and are lost altogether; perhaps by desperate galloping, they may head them off, get them running in a circle, and finally stop them. Once stopped, they may break again, and possibly divide up, one cowboy, perhaps, following each band. I have known six such stops and renewed stampedes to take place in one night, the cowboy staying with his ever-diminishing herd of steers until daybreak, when he managed to get them under control again, and, by careful humoring of his jaded, staggering horse, finally brought those there were left back to the camp, several miles distant. The riding in these night stampedes is wild and dangerous to a degree, especially if the man gets caught in the rush of the beasts. It also frequently necessitates an immense amount of work in collecting the scattered animals. On one such occasion a small party of us were thirty-six hours in the saddle, dismounting only to change horses or to eat. We were almost worn out at the end of the time; but it must be kept in mind that for a long spell of such work a stock-saddle is far less tiring then the ordinary Eastern or English one, and in every way superior to it.

By very hard riding, such a stampede may sometimes be prevented. Once we were bringing a thousand head of young cattle down to my lower ranch, and as the river was high were obliged to take the inland trail. The third night we were forced to make a dry camp, the cattle having had no water since the morning. Nevertheless, we got them bedded down without difficulty, and one of the cowboys and myself stood first guard. But very soon after nightfall, when the darkness had become complete, the thirsty brutes of one accord got on their feet and tried to break out. The only salvation was to keep them close together, as, if they once got scattered, we knew they could never be gathered; so I kept on one side, and the cowboy on the other, and never in my life did I ride so hard. In the darkness I could but dimly see the shadowy outlines of the herd, as with whip and spurs I ran the pony along its edge, turning back the beasts at one point barely in time to wheel and keep them in at another. The ground was cut up by numerous little gullies, and each of us got several falls, horses and riders turning complete somersaults. We were dripping with sweat, and our ponies quivering and trembling like quaking aspens when, after more than an hour of the most violent exertion, we finally got the herd quieted again.

On another occasion while with the round-up we were spared an excessively unpleasant night only because there happened to be two or three great corrals not more than a mile or so away. All day long it had been raining heavily, and we were well drenched; but towards evening it lulled a little, and the day herd, a very large one, of some two thousand head, was gathered on an open bottom. We had turned the horses loose, and in our oilskin slickers cowered, soaked and comfortless, under the lee of the wagon, to take a meal of damp bread and lukewarm tea, the sizzling embers of the fire having about given up the ghost after a fruitless struggle with the steady downpour. Suddenly the wind began to come in quick, sharp gusts, and soon a regular blizzard was blowing, driving the rain in stinging level sheets before it. Just as we were preparing to turn into bed, with the certainty of a night of more or less chilly misery ahead of us, one of my men, an iron-faced personage, whom no one would ever have dreamed had a weakness for poetry, looked towards the plain where the cattle were, and remarked, "I guess there's 'racing and chasing on Cannobie Lea' now, sure." Following his gaze, I saw that the cattle had begun to drift before the storm, the night guards being evidently unable to cope with them, while at the other wagons riders were saddling in hot haste and spurring off to their help through the blinding rain. Some of us at once ran out to our own saddle-band. All of the ponies were standing huddled together, with their heads down and their tails to the wind. They were wild and restive enough usually; but the storm had cowed them, and we were able to catch them without either rope or halter. We made quick work of saddling; and the second each man was ready, away he loped through the dusk, splashing and slipping in the pools of water that studded the muddy plain. Most of the riders were already out when we arrived. The cattle were gathered in a compact, wedge-shaped, or rather fan-shaped mass, with their tails to the wind—that is, towards the thin end of the wedge or fan. In front of this fan-shaped mass of frightened, maddened beats was a long line of cowboys, each muffled in his slicker and with his broad hat pulled down over his eyes, to shield him from the pelting rain. When the cattle were quiet for a moment every horseman at once turned round with his back to the wind, and the whole line stood as motionless as so many sentries. Then, if the cattle began to spread out and overlap at the ends, or made a rush and broke through at one part of the lines, there would be a change into wild activity. The men, shouting and swaying in their saddles, darted to and fro with reckless speed, utterly heedless of danger—now racing to the threatened point, now checking and wheeling their horses so sharply as to bring them square on their haunches, or even throw them flat down, while the hoofs plowed long furrows in the slippery soil, until, after some minutes of this mad galloping hither and thither, the herd, having drifted a hundred yards or so, would be once more brought up standing. We always had to let them drift a little to prevent their spreading out too much. The din of the thunder was terrific, peal following peal until they mingled in one continuous, rumbling roar; and at every thunder-clap louder than its fellows the cattle would try to break away. Darkness had set in, but each flash of lightning showed us a dense array of tossing horns and staring eyes. It grew always harder to hold in the herd; but the drift took us along to the corrals already spoken of, whose entrances were luckily to windward. As soon as we reached the first we cut off part of the herd, and turned it within; and after again doing this with the second, we were able to put all the remaining animals into the third. The instant the cattle were housed five-sixth of the horsemen started back at full speed for the wagons; the rest of us barely waited to put up the bars and make the corrals secure before galloping after them. We had to ride right in the teeth of the driving storm; and once at the wagons we made small delay in crawling under our blankets, damp though the latter were, for we were ourselves far too wet, stiff, and cold not to hail with grateful welcome any kind of shelter from the wind and the rain.

All animals were benumbed by the violence of this gale of cold rain: a prairie chicken rose from under my horse's feet so heavily that, thoughtlessly striking at it, I cut it down with my whip; while when a jack rabbit got up ahead of us, it was barely able to limp clumsily out of our way.

But though there is much work and hardship, rough fare, monotony, and exposure connected with the round-up, yet there are few men who do not look forward to it and back to it with pleasure. The only fault to be found is that the hours of work are so long that one does not usually have enough time to sleep. The food, if rough, is good; beef, bread, pork, beans, coffee or tea, always canned tomatoes, and often rice, canned corn, or sauce made from dried apples. The men are good-humored, bold and thoroughly interested in their business, continually vying with one another in the effort to see which can do the work best. It is superbly health-giving, and is full of excitement and adventure, calling for the exhibition of pluck, self-reliance, hardihood, and dashing horsemanship; and of all forms of physical labor the earliest and pleasantest is to sit in the saddle.

CHAPTER ELEVEN

A MEXICAN PLUG

Mark Twain

I resolved to have a horse to ride. I had never seen such wild, free, magnificent horsemanship outside of a circus as these picturesquely-clad Mexicans, Californians and Mexicanized Americans displayed in Carson streets every day. How they rode! Leaning just gently forward out of the perpendicular, easy and nonchalant, with broad slouch-hat brim blown square up in front, and long *riata* swinging above the head, they swept through the town like the wind! The next minute they were only a sailing puff of dust on the far desert. If they trotted, they sat up gallantly and gracefully, and seemed part of the horse; did not go jiggering up and down after the silly Miss-Nancy fashion of the riding-schools. I had quickly learned to tell a horse from a cow, and was full of anxiety to learn more. I was resolved to buy a horse.

While the thought was rankling in my mind, the auctioneer came skurrying through the plaza on a black beast that had as many humps and corners on him as a dromedary, and was necessarily uncomely; but he was "going, going, at twenty-two!—a horse, saddle and bridle at twenty-two dollars, gentlemen!" and I could hardly resist.

A man whom I did not know (he turned out to be the auctioneer's brother) noticed the wistful look in my eye, and observed that that was a very remarkable horse to be going at such a price; and added that the saddle alone was worth the money. It was a Spanish saddle, with ponderous *tapidaros*, and furnished with the ungainly sole-leather covering with the unspellable name. I said I had half a notion to bid. Then this keen-eyed person appeared to me to be "taking my measure"; but I dismissed the suspicion when he spoke, for his manner was full of guileless candor and truthfulness. Said he:

"I know that horse—know him well. You are a stranger, I take it, and so you might think he was an American horse, but I assure you he is not. He is nothing of the kind; but—excuse my speaking in a low voice, other people being near—he is, without the shadow of a doubt, a Genuine Mexican Plug!"

I did not know what a Genuine Mexican Plug was, but there was something about this man's way of saying it, that made me swear inwardly that I would own a Genuine Mexican Plug, or die.

"Has he any other—er—advantages?" I inquired, suppressing what eagerness I could.

He hooked his forefinger in the pocket of my army-shirt, led me to one side, and breathed in my ear impressively these words:

"He can out-buck anything in America!"

"Going, going, going—at *twenty*-four dollars and a half, gen—"

"Twenty-seven!" I shouted in a frenzy.

"And sold!" said the auctioneer, and passed over the Genuine Mexican Plug to me.

I could scarcely contain my exultation. I paid the money, and put the animal in a neighboring livery-stable to dine and rest himself.

In the afternoon I brought the creature into the plaza, and certain citizens held him by the head, and others by the tail, while I mounted him. As soon as they let go, he placed all his feet in a bunch together, lowered his back, and then suddenly arched it upward, and shot me straight into the air a matter of three or four feet! I came as straight down again, lit in the saddle, went instantly up again, came down almost on the high pommel, shot up again, and came down on the horse's neck—all in the space of three or four seconds. Then he rose and stood almost straight up on his hind feet, and I, clasping his lean neck desperately, slid back into the saddle, and held on. He came down, and immediately hoisted his heels into the air, delivering a vicious kick at the sky, and stood on his forefeet. And then down he came once more, and began the original exercise of shooting me straight up again. The third time I went up I heard a stranger say:

"Oh, *don't* he buck, though!"

While I was up, somebody struck the horse a sounding thwack with a leathern strap, and when I arrived again the Genuine Mexican Plug was not there. A Californian youth chased him up and caught him, and asked if he might have a ride. I granted him that luxury. He mounted the Genuine, got lifted into the air once, but sent his spurs home as he descended, and the horse darted away like a telegram.

He soared over three fences like a bird, and disappeared down the road toward the Washoe Valley.

I sat down on a stone, with a sigh, and by a natural impulse one of my hands sought my forehead, and the other the base of my stomach. I believe I never appreciated, till then, the poverty of the human machinery—for I still needed a hand or two to place elsewhere. Pen cannot describe how I was jolted up. Imagination cannot conceive how disjointed I was—how internally, externally and universally I was unsettled, mixed up and ruptured. There was a sympathetic crowd around me, though.

One elderly-looking comforter said:

"Stranger, you've been taken in. Everybody in this camp knows that horse. Any child, any Injun, could have told you that he'd buck; he is the very worst devil to buck on the continent of America. You hear *me*. I'm Curry. *Old* Curry. Old *Abe* Curry. And moreover, he is a simon-pure, out-and-out genuine d—d Mexican plug, and an uncommon mean one at that, too. Why, you turnip, if you had laid low and kept dark, there's chances to buy an *American* horse for mighty little more than you paid for that bloody old foreign relic."

I gave no sign; but I made up my mind that if the auctioneer's brother's funeral took place while I was in the Territory I would postpone all other recreations and attend it.

After a gallop of sixteen miles the Californian youth and the Genuine Mexican Plug came tearing into town again, shedding foam-flakes like the spume-spray that drives before a typhoon, and, with one final skip over a wheelbarrow and a Chinaman, cast anchor in front of the "ranch."

Such panting and blowing! Such spreading and contracting of the red equine nostrils, and glaring of the wild equine eye! But was the imperial beast subjugated? Indeed he was not. His lordship the Speaker of the House thought he was, and mounted him to go down to the Capitol; but the first dash the creature made was over a pile of telegraph poles half as high as a church; and his time to the Capitol—one mile and three quarters—remains unbeaten to this day. But then he took an advantage—he left out the mile, and only did the three quarters. That is to say, he made a straight cut across lots, preferring fences and ditches to a crooked road; and when the Speaker got to the Capitol he said he had been in the air so much he felt as if he had made the trip on a comet.

In the evening the Speaker came home afoot for exercise, and got the Genuine towed back behind a quartz wagon. The next day I loaned the animal to the Clerk of the House to go down to the Dana silver mine, six miles, and *he* walked back for exercise, and got the horse towed. Everybody I loaned him to always walked back; they never could get enough exercise any other way. Still, I continued to loan him to anybody who was willing to borrow him, my idea being to get him crippled, and throw him on the borrower's hands, or killed, and make the borrower pay for him, but somehow nothing ever happened to him. He took chances that no other horse ever took and survived, but he always came out safe. It was his daily habit to try experiments that had always before been considered impossible, but he always got through. Sometimes he miscalculated a little, and did not get his rider through intact, but *he* always got through himself. Of course I had tried to sell him; but that was a stretch of simplicity which met with little sympathy. The auctioneer stormed up and down the streets for four days, dispersing the populace, interrupting business, and destroying children, and never got a bid—at least never any but the eighteen-dollar one he hired a notoriously substanceless bummer to make. The people only smiled pleasantly, and restrained their desire to buy, if they had any. Then the auctioneer brought in his bill, and I withdrew the horse from the market. We tried to trade him off at private vendue next, offering him at a sacrifice for second-hand tombstones, old iron, temperance tracts—any kind of property. But holders were stiff, and we retired from the market again. I never tried to ride the horse any more. Walking was good enough exercise for a man like me, that had nothing the matter with him except ruptures, internal injuries, and such things. Finally I tried to *give* him away. But it was a failure. Parties said earthquakes were handy enough on the Pacific coast—they did not wish to own one. As a last resort I offered him to the Governor for the use of the "Brigade." His face lit up eagerly at first, but toned down again, and he said the thing would be too palpable.

Just then the livery stable man brought in his bill for six weeks' keeping—stall-room for the horse, fifteen dollars; hay for the horse, two hundred and fifty! The Genuine Mexican Plug had eaten a ton of the article, and the man said he would have eaten a hundred if he had let him.

I will remark here, in all seriousness, that the regular price of hay during that year and a part of the next was really two hundred and fifty dollars a ton. During a part of the previous year it had sold at five hundred a ton, in gold, and during the winter before that there was such scarcity of the article that in several instances small quantities had brought eight hundred dollars a ton in coin! The consequence might be guessed without my telling it; people turned their stock loose to starve, and before the spring arrived Carson and Eagle valleys were almost literally carpeted with their carcases! Any old settler there will verify these statements.

I managed to pay the livery bill, and that same day I gave the Genuine Mexican Plug to a passing Arkansas emigrant whom fortune delivered into my hand. If this ever meets his eye, he will doubtless remember the donation.

Now whoever has had the luck to ride a real Mexican plug will recognize the animal depicted in this chapter, and hardly consider him exaggerated—but the uninitiated will feel justified in regarding his portrait as a fancy sketch, perhaps.

CHAPTER TWELVE

ON THE TRAIL

Zane Gray

S hefford was awakened next morning by a sound he had never heard before—the plunging of hobbled horses on soft turf. It was clear daylight, with a ruddy color in the sky and a tinge of red along the cañon rim. He saw Withers, Lake, and the Indian driving the mustangs toward camp.

The burros appeared lazy, yet willing. But the mustangs and the mule Withers called Red and the gray mare Dynamite were determined not to be driven into camp. It was astonishing how much action they had, how much ground they could cover with their forefeet hobbled together. They were exceedingly skilful; they lifted both forefeet at once, and then plunged. And they all went in different directions. Nas Ta Bega darted in here and there to head off escape.

Shefford pulled on his boots and went out to help. He got too close to the gray mare and, warned by a yell from Withers, he jumped back just in time to avoid her vicious heels. Then Shefford turned his attention to Nack-yal and chased him all over the flat in a futile effort to catch him. Nas Ta Bega came to Shefford's assistance and put a rope over Nack-yal's head.

"Don't ever get behind one of these mustangs," said Withers, warningly, as Shefford came up. "You might be killed. . . . Eat your bite now. We'll soon be out of here."

Shefford had been late in awakening. The others had breakfasted. He found eating somewhat difficult in the excitement that ensued. Nas Ta Bega held ropes which were round the necks of Red and Dynamite. The mule showed his cunning and always appeared to present his heels to Withers, who tried to approach him with a pack-saddle. The patience of the trader was a revelation to Shefford. And at length Red was cornered by the three men, the pack-saddle was strapped on, and then the packs. Red promptly bucked the packs off, and the work had to be done over again. Then Red dropped his long ears and seemed ready to be tractable.

When Shefford turned his attention to Dynamite he decided that this was his first sight of a wild horse. The gray mare had fiery eyes that rolled and showed the white. She jumped straight up, screamed, pawed, bit, and then plunged down to shoot her hind hoofs into the air as high as her head had been. She was amazingly agile and she seemed mad to kill something. She dragged the Indian about, and when Joe Lake got a rope on her hind foot she dragged them both. They lashed her with the ends of the lassoes, which action only made her kick harder. She plunged into camp, drove Shefford flying for his life, knocked down two of the burros, and played havoc with the unstrapped packs. Withers ran to the assistance of Lake, and the two of them hauled back with all their strength and weight. They were both powerful and heavy men. Dynamite circled round and finally, after kicking the camp-fire to bits, fell down on her haunches in the hot embers. "Let—her—set—there!" panted Withers. And Joe Lake shouted, "Burn up, you durn coyote!" Both men appeared delighted that she had brought upon herself just punishment. Dynamite sat in the remains of the fire long enough to get burnt, and then she got up and meekly allowed Withers to throw a tarpaulin and a roll of blankets over her and tie them fast.

Lake and Withers were sweating freely when this job was finished.

"Say, is that a usual morning's task with the pack-animals?" asked Shefford.

"They're all pretty decent to-day, except Dynamite," replied Withers. "She's got to be worked out."

Shefford felt both amusement and consternation. The sun was just rising over the ramparts of the cañon, and he had already seen more difficult and dangerous work accomplished than half a dozen men of his type could do in a whole day. He liked the outlook of his new duty as Withers's assistant, but he felt helplessly inefficient. Still, all he needed was experience. He passed over what he anticipated would be pain and peril—the cost was of no moment.

Soon the pack-train was on the move, with the Indian leading. This morning Nack-yal began his strange swinging off to the left, precisely as he had done the day before. It got to be annoying to Shefford, and he lost patience with the mustang and jerked him sharply round. This, however, had no great effect upon Nack-yal.

As the train headed straight up the cañon Joe Lake dropped back to ride beside Shefford. The Mormon had been amiable and friendly.

"Flock of deer up that draw," he said, pointing up a narrow side cañon.

Shefford gazed to see a half-dozen small, brown, long-eared objects, very like burros, watching the pack-train pass.

"Are they deer?" he asked, delightedly.

"Sure are," replied Joe, sincerely. "Get down and shoot one. There's a rifle in your saddle-sheath."

Shefford had already discovered that he had been armed this morning, a matter which had caused him reflection. These animals certainly looked like deer; he had seen a few deer, though not in their native wild haunts; and he experienced the thrill of the hunter. Dismounting, he drew the rifle out of the sheath and started toward the little cañon.

"Hyar! Where you going with that gun?" yelled Withers. "That's a bunch of burros. . . . Joe's up to his old tricks. Shefford, look out for Joe!"

Rather sheepishly Shefford returned to his mustang and sheathed the rifle, and then took a long look at the animals up the draw. They resembled deer, but upon second glance they surely were burros.

"Durn me! Now if I didn't think they sure were deer!" exclaimed Joe. He appeared absolutely sincere and innocent. Shefford hardly knew how to take this likable Mormon, but vowed he would be on his guard in the future.

Nas Ta Bega soon led the pack-train toward the left wall of the cañon, and evidently intended to scale it. Shefford could not see any trail, and the wall appeared steep and insurmountable. But upon nearing the cliff he saw a narrow broken trail leading zigzag up over smooth rock, weathered slope, and through cracks.

"Spread out, and careful now!" yelled Withers.

The need of both advices soon became manifest to Shefford. The burros started stones rolling, making danger for those below. Shefford dismounted and led Nack-yal and turned aside many a rolling rock. The Indian and the burros, with the red mule leading, climbed steadily. But the mustangs had trouble. Joe's spirited bay had to be coaxed to face the ascent; Nack-yal balked at every difficult step; and Dynamite slipped on a flat slant of rock and slid down forty feet. Withers and Lake with ropes hauled the mare out of the dangerous position. Shefford, who brought up the rear, saw all the action, and it was exciting, but his pleasure in the climb was spoiled by sight of blood and hair on the stones. The ascent was crooked, steep, and long, and when Shefford reached the top of the wall he was glad to rest. It made him gasp to look down and see what he had surmounted. The cañon floor, green and level, lay a thousand feet below; and the wild burros which had followed on the trail looked like rabbits.

Shefford mounted presently, and rode out upon a wide, smooth trail leading into a cedar forest. There were bunches of gray sage in the open places. The air was cool and crisp, laden with a sweet fragrance. He saw Lake and Withers bobbing along, now on one side of the trail, now on the other, and they kept to a steady trot. Occasionally the Indian and his bright-red saddle-blanket showed in an opening of the cedars.

It was level country, and there was nothing for Shefford to see except cedar and sage, an outcropping of red rock in places, and the winding trail. Mocking-birds made melody everywhere. Shefford seemed full of a strange pleasure, and the hours flew by. Nack-yal still wanted to be everlastingly turning off the trail, and, moreover, now he wanted to go faster. He was eager, restless, dissatisfied.

At noon the pack-train descended into a deep draw, well covered with cedar and sage. There was plenty of grass and shade, but no water. Shefford was surprised to see that every pack was removed; however, the roll of blankets was left on Dynamite.

The men made a fire and began to cook a noonday meal. Shefford, tired and warm, sat in a shady spot and watched. He had become all eyes. He had almost forgotten Fay Larkin; he had forgotten his trouble; and the present seemed sweet and full. Presently his ears were filled by a pattering roar and, looking up the draw, he saw two streams of sheep and goats coming down. Soon an Indian shepherd appeared, riding a fine mustang. A cream-colored colt bounded along behind, and presently a shaggy dog came in sight. The Indian dismounted at the camp, and his flock spread by in two white and black streams. The dog went with them. Withers and Joe shook hands with the Indian, whom Joe called "Navvy," and Shefford lost no time in doing likewise. Then Nas Ta Bega came in, and he and the Navajo talked. When the meal was ready all of them sat down round the canvas. The shepherd did not tie his horse.

Presently Shefford noticed that Nack-yal had returned to camp and was acting strangely. Evidently he was attracted by the Indian's mustang or the cream-colored colt. At any rate, Nack-yal hung around, tossed his head, whinnied in a low, nervous manner, and looked strangely eager and wild. Shefford was at first amused, then curious. Nack-yal approached too close to the mother of the colt, and she gave him a sounding kick in the ribs. Nack-yal uttered a plaintive snort and backed away, to stand, crestfallen, with all his eagerness and fire vanished.

Nas Ta Bega pointed to the mustang and said something in his own tongue. Then Withers addressed the visiting Indian, and they exchanged some words, whereupon the trader turned to Shefford.

"I bought Nack-yal from this Indian three years ago. This mare is Nack-yal's mother. He was born over here to the south. That's why he always swung left off the trail. He wanted to go home. Just now he recognized his mother and she whaled away and gave him a whack for his pains. She's got a colt now and probably didn't recognize Nack-yal. But he's broken-hearted."

The trader laughed, and Joe said, "You can't tell what these durn mustangs will do." Shefford felt sorry for Nack-yal, and when it came time to saddle him again found him easier to handle than ever before. Nack-yal stood with head down, broken-spirited.

Shefford was the first to ride up out of the draw, and once upon the top of the ridge he halted to gaze, wide-eyed and entranced. A rolling, endless plain sloped down beneath him, and led him on to a distant round-topped mountain. To the right a red cañon opened its jagged jaws, and away to the north rose a whorled and strange sea of curved ridges, crags, and domes.

Nas Ta Bega rode up then, leading the pack-train.

"Bi Nai, that is Na-tsis-an," he said, pointing to the mountain. "Navajo Mountain. And there in the north are the cañons."

Shefford followed the Indian down the trail and soon lost sight of that wide green-and-red wilderness. Nas Ta Bega turned at an intersecting trail, rode down into the cañon, and climbed out on the other side. Shefford got a glimpse now and then of the black dome of the mountain, but for the most part the distant points of the country were hidden. They crossed many trails, and went up and down the sides of many shallow cañons. Troops of wild mustangs whistled at them, stood on ridge-tops to watch, and then dashed away with manes and tails flying.

Withers rode forward presently and halted the pack-train. He had some conversation with Nas Ta Bega, whereupon the Indian turned his horse and trotted back, to disappear in the cedars.

"I'm some worried," explained Withers. "Joe thinks he saw a bunch of horsemen trailing us. My eyes are bad and I can't see far. The Indian will find out. I took a roundabout way to reach the village because I'm always dodging Shadd." This communication lent an added zest to the journey. Shefford could hardly believe the truth that his eyes and his ears brought to his consciousness. He turned in behind Withers and rode down the rough trail, helping the mustang all in his power. It occurred to him that Nack-yal had been entirely different since that meeting with his mother in the draw. He turned no more off the trail; he answered readily to the rein; he did not look afar from every ridge. Shefford conceived a liking for the mustang.

Withers turned sidewise in his saddle and let his mustang pick the way.

"Another time we'll go up round the base of the mountain, where you can look down on the grandest scene in the world," said he. "Two hundred miles of wind-worn rock, all smooth and bare, without a single straight line—cañons, caves, bridges—the most wonderful country in the world! Even the Indians haven't explored it. It's haunted, for them, and they have strange gods. The Navajos will hunt on this side of the mountain, but not on the other. That north side is consecrated ground. My wife has long been trying to get the Navajos to tell her the secret of Nonnezoshe. Nonnezoshe means Rainbow Bridge. The Indians worship it, but as far as she can find out only a few have ever seen it. I imagine it 'd be worth some trouble."

"Maybe that's the bridge Venters talked about—the one overarching the entrance to Surprise Valley," said Shefford.

"It might be," replied the trader. "You've got a good chance of finding out. Nas Ta Bega is the man. You stick to that Indian. . . . Well, we start down here into this cañon, and we go down *some,* I reckon.

In half an hour you'll see sago-lilies and Indian paint-brush and ver-
milion cactus."

About the middle of the afternoon the pack-train and its drivers
arrived at the hidden Mormon village. Nas Ta Bega had not returned
from his scout back along the trail.

Shefford's sensibilities had all been overstrained, but he had left
in him enthusiasm and appreciation that made the situation of this
village a fairyland. It was a valley, a cañon floor, so long that he could
not see the end, and perhaps a quarter of a mile wide. The air was
hot, still, and sweetly odorous of unfamiliar flowers. Piñon and cedar
trees surrounded the little log and stone houses, and along the walls of
the cañon stood sharp-pointed, dark-green spruce-trees. These walls
were singular of shape and color. They were not imposing in height,
but they waved like the long, undulating swell of a sea. Every foot of
surface was perfectly smooth, and the long curved lines of darker tinge
that streaked the red followed the rounded line of the slope at the top.
Far above, yet overhanging, were great yellow crags and peaks, and
between these, still higher, showed the pine-fringed slope of Navajo
Mountain with snow in the sheltered places, and glistening streams,
like silver threads, running down.

All this Shefford noticed as he entered the valley from round a
corner of wall. Upon nearer view he saw and heard a host of children,
who, looking up to see the intruders, scattered like frightened quail.
Long gray grass covered the ground, and here and there wide, smooth
paths had been worn. A swift and murmuring brook ran through the
middle of the valley, and its banks were bordered with flowers.

Withers led the way to one side near the wall, where a clump of
cedar-trees and a dark, swift spring boiling out of the rocks and banks
of amber moss with purple blossoms made a beautiful camp site. Here

the mustangs were unsaddled and turned loose without hobbles. It was certainly unlikely that they would leave such a spot. Some of the burros were unpacked, and the others Withers drove off into the village.

"Sure's pretty nice," said Joe, wiping his sweaty face. "I'll never want to leave. It suits me to lie on this moss. . . . Take a drink of that spring."

Shefford complied with alacrity and found the water cool and sweet, and he seemed to feel it all through him. Then he returned to the mossy bank. He did not reply to Joe. In fact, all his faculties were absorbed in watching and feeling, and he lay there long after Joe went off to the village. The murmur of water, the hum of bees, the songs of strange birds, the sweet, warm air, the dreamy summer somnolence of the valley—all these added drowsiness to Shefford's weary lassitude, and he fell asleep. When he awoke Nas Ta Bega was sitting near him and Joe was busy near a camp-fire.

"Hello, Nas Ta Bega!" said Shefford. "Was there any one trailing us?"

The Navajo nodded.

Joe raised his head and with forceful brevity said, "Shadd."

"Shadd!" echoed Shefford, remembering the dark, sinister face of his visitor that night in the Sagi. "Joe, is it serious—his trailing us?"

"Well, I don't know how durn serious it is, but I'm scared to death," replied Lake. "He and his gang will hold us up somewhere on the way home."

Shefford regarded Joe with both concern and doubt. Joe's words were at variance with his looks.

"Say, pard, can you shoot a rifle?" queried Joe.

"Yes. I'm a fair shot at targets."

The Mormon nodded his head as if pleased. "That's good. These outlaws are all poor shots with a rifle. So'm I. But I can handle a six-shooter. I reckon we'll make Shadd sweat if he pushes us."

Withers returned, driving the burros, all of which had been unpacked down to the saddles. Two gray-bearded men accompanied him. One of them appeared to be very old and venerable, and walked with a stick. The other had a sad-lined face and kind, mild blue eyes. Shefford observed that Lake seemed unusually respectful. Withers introduced these Mormons merely as Smith and Henninger. They were very cordial and pleasant in their greetings to Shefford. Presently another, somewhat younger, man joined the group, a stalwart, jovial fellow with ruddy face. There was certainly no mistaking his kindly welcome as he shook Shefford's hand. His name was Beal. The three stood round the camp-fire for a while, evidently glad of the presence of fellow-men and to hear news from the outside. Finally they went away, taking Joe with them. Withers took up the task of getting supper where Joe had been made to leave it.

"Shefford, listen," he said, presently, as he knelt before the fire. "I told them right out that you'd been a Gentile clergyman—that you'd gone back on your religion. It impressed them and you've been well received. I'll tell the same thing over at Stonebridge. You'll get in right. Of course I don't expect they'll make a Mormon of you. But they'll try to. Meanwhile you can be square and friendly all the time you're trying to find your Fay Larkin. To-morrow you'll meet some of the women. They're good souls, but, like any women, crazy for news. Think what it is to be shut up in here between these walls!"

"Withers, I'm intensely interested," replied Shefford, "and excited, too. Shall we stay here long?"

"I'll stay a couple of days, then go to Stonebridge with Joe. He'll come back here, and when you both feel like leaving, and if Nas Ta Bega thinks it safe, you'll take a trail over to some Indian hogans and pack me out a load of skins and blankets. . . . My boy, you've all the time there is, and I wish you luck. This isn't a bad place to loaf. I always get sentimental over here. Maybe it's the women. Some of them are pretty, and one of them—Shefford, they call her the Sago Lily. Her first name is Mary, I'm told. Don't know her last name. She's lovely. And I'll bet you forget Fay Larkin in a flash. Only—be careful. You drop in here with rather peculiar credentials, so to speak—as my helper and as a man with no religion! You'll not only be fully trusted, but you'll be welcome to these lonely women. So be careful. Remember it's my secret belief they are sealed wives and are visited occasionally at night by their husbands. I don't *know* this, but I believe it. And you're not supposed to dream of that."

"How many men in the village?" asked Shefford.

"Three. You met them."

"Have they wives?" asked Shefford, curiously.

"Wives! Well, I guess. But only one each that I know of. Joe Lake is the only unmarried Mormon I've met."

"And no men—strangers, cowboys, outlaws—ever come to this village?"

"Except to Indians, it seems to be a secret so far," replied the trader, earnestly. "But it can't be kept secret. I've said that time after time over in Stonebridge. With Mormons it's 'sufficient unto the day is the evil thereof.'"

"What 'll happen when outsiders do learn and ride in here?"

"There'll be trouble—maybe bloodshed. Mormon women are absolutely good, but they're human, and want and need a little life. And, strange to say, Mormon men are pig-headedly jealous. . . . Why, if some of the cowboys I knew in Durango would ride over here there'd simply be hell. But that's a long way, and probably this village will be deserted before news of it ever reaches Colorado. There's more danger of Shadd and his gang coming in. Shadd's half Piute. He must know of this place. And he's got some white outlaws in his gang. . . . Come on. Grub's ready, and I'm too hungry to talk."

Later, when shadows began to gather in the valley and the lofty peaks above were gold in the sunset glow, Withers left camp to look after the straying mustangs, and Shefford strolled to and fro under the cedars. The lights and shades in the Sagi that first night had moved him to enthusiastic watchfulness, but here they were so weird and beautiful that he was enraptured. He actually saw great shafts of gold and shadows of purple streaming from the peaks down into the valley. It was day on the heights and twilight in the valley. The swiftly changing colors were like rainbows.

While he strolled up and down several women came to the spring and filled their buckets. They wore shawls or hoods and their garments were somber, but, nevertheless, they appeared to have youth and comeliness. They saw him, looked at him curiously, and then, without speaking, went back on the well-trodden path. Presently down the path appeared a woman—a girl in lighter garb. It was almost white. She was shapely and walked with free, graceful step, reminding him of the Indian girl, Glen Naspa. This one wore a hood shaped like a huge sunbonnet and it concealed her face. She carried a bucket. When she reached the spring and went down the few stone steps Shefford saw that she did not have on shoes. As she braced herself to lift the bucket her bare foot clung to the mossy stone. It was a strong, sinewy, beautiful foot, instinct with youth. He was curious enough, he thought, but the awakening artist in him made him more so. She dragged at the full bucket and had difficulty in lifting it out of the hole. Shefford strode forward and took the bucket-handle from her.

"Won't you let me help you?" he said, lifting the bucket. "Indeed—it's very heavy."

"Oh—thank you," she said, without raising her head. Her voice seemed singularly young and sweet. He had not heard a voice like it. She moved down the path and he walked beside her. He felt embarrassed, yet more curious than ever; he wanted to say something, to turn and look at her, but he kept on for a dozen paces without making up his mind.

Finally he said: "Do you really carry this heavy bucket? Why, it makes my arm ache."

"Twice every day—morning and evening," she replied. "I'm very strong."

Then he stole a look out of the corner of his eye, and, seeing that her face was hidden from him by the hood, he turned to observe her at better advantage. A long braid of hair hung down her back. In the twilight it gleamed dull gold. She came up to his shoulder. The sleeve nearest him was rolled up to her elbow, revealing a fine round arm. Her hand, like her foot, was brown, strong, and well shaped. It was a hand that had been developed by labor. She was full-bosomed, yet slender, and she walked with a free stride that made Shefford admire and wonder.

They passed several of the little stone and log houses, and women greeted them as they went by, and children peered shyly from the doors. He kept trying to think of something to say, and, failing in that, determined to have one good look under the hood before he left her.

"You walk lame," she said, solicitously. "Let me carry the bucket now—please. My house is near."

"Am I lame? . . . Guess so, a little," he replied. "It was a hard ride for me. But I'll carry the bucket just the same."

They went on under some piñon-trees, down a path to a little house identical with the others, except that it had a stone porch. Shefford smelled fragrant wood-smoke and saw a column curling from the low, flat, stone chimney. Then he set the bucket down on the porch.

"Thank you, Mr. Shefford," she said.

"You know my name?" he asked.

"Yes. Mr. Withers spoke to my nearest neighbor and she told me."

"Oh, I see. And you—"

He did not go on and she did not reply. When she stepped upon the porch and turned he was able to see under the hood. The face there was in shadow, and for that very reason he answered to ungovernable impulse and took a step closer to her. Dark, grave, sad eyes looked down at him, and he felt as if he could never draw his own glance away. He seemed not to see the rest of her face, and yet felt that it was lovely. Then a downward movement of the hood hid from him the strange eyes and the shadowy loveliness.

"I—I beg your pardon," he said, quickly, drawing back. "I'm rude. . . . Withers told me about a girl he called—he said looked like a sago-lily. That's no excuse to stare under your hood. But I—I was curious. I wondered if—"

He hesitated, realizing how foolish his talk was. She stood a moment, probably watching him, but he could not be sure, for her face was hidden.

"They call me that," she said. "But my name is Mary."

"Mary—what ?" he asked.

"Just Mary," she said, simply. "Good night."

He did not say good night and could not have told why. She took up the bucket and went into the dark house. Shefford hurried away into the gathering darkness.